Reenita Malhotra Hora is an award-winning broadcast journalist, Ayurveda clinician and author of books on Ayurveda and finance. Her debut fiction novel, *Operation Mom: How I Got My Mother a Life and Man* has been recognised as a must-read young adult book written by an Indian author. *When Arya Fell Through the Fault* is her second release in this genre.

Reenita anchors Hong Kong's popular morning finance programme, *Money for Nothing* on RTHK Radio 3. Her weekend storytelling show, *Asian Threads* has won her a gold trophy at the New York Festivals International Radio Program Awards.

Native to Mumbai, she currently lives with her family in Hong Kong. You can follow her on Twitter (@reenymal) and Facebook (https://www.facebook.com/ReenitaMalhotraHora) or visit her online at www.reenita.com.

When Arya Fell Through the Fault

Reenita Malhotra Hora

OM
Om Books International

First Published in 2015 by

OM
Om Books International

An imprint of Om Books International
Corporate & Editorial Office
A 12, Sector 64, Noida 201 301
Uttar Pradesh, India
Phone: +91 120 477 4100
Email: editorial@ombooks.com
Website: www.ombooksinternational.com

Sales Office
107, Darya Ganj, New Delhi 110 002, India
Phone: +91 11 4000 9000, 2326 3363, 2326 5303
Fax: +91 11 2327 8091
Email: sales@ombooks.com
Website: www.ombooks.com

ISBN : 978-93-81607-62-6

Printed in India

10 9 8 7 6 5 4 3 2 1

For *Arya Vir Hora*

who inspires the dream of eternal childhood

Contents

Prologue

Last night, I dreamt I was fighting with Ravana again!

I zoomed in towards the demon king on my skateboard, shooting arrows, one by one, at each of his ten heads. There's nothing I hated more than those hideous heads with their whopping piggy lips, crooked yellow teeth and oozing zits.

Each night in her stories from the Ramayana, Ma would describe Ravana, the most sinister demon who existed to vanquish good. But lately in my dreams, he looked more like a pig-faced pre-teen with bad dental hygiene. Why couldn't I get rid of this ugh-ster?

I sped down San Francisco's side streets on my skateboard charging at his heads, but, each time I knocked one off, another simply grew in its place. I swivelled my skateboard around looking for a better angle to zero in from. Alas, no such luck. Ravana thrust his chest towards me with a sneer, reeking of what must have been yesterday's breakfast. 'Heard of something called dental floss, goopeater?'

Uggh! There was the label.

'Goopeating terrorist!' he sneered, grabbing my lunch bag out of nowhere.

Wait a minute, I was the terrorist?

Then, the worst happened. The demon king hurled the contents of my lunch bag at me. Projectiles of khichdi invaded my airspace. Within moments, Ravana had splattered my goopy lunch all over the dashboard of my dreams. One tablespoonful came hurtling towards me, landing right between my eyes. It pushed me off the edge of some unknown crevice into an abyss of darkness. Once again, I fell deeper... and deeper...and deeper into nothing.

I woke up in a cold sweat. The fear of falling through emptiness had been a deep-seated insecurity since my childhood days. As I stared up at the crown moldings on my bedroom walls, I could see that once again, Ravana had sucked me into the dark depths of emptiness, using Ma's home-cooked meal as a weapon.

Dang it! I stood no chance against demons, not as long as I was a goopeating terrorist.

Arya Bin Laden

The day I was first called a goopeater was the worst day of my life, until the next day and the day after that.

Not that I couldn't handle insults. On the contrary, I'd grown so used to the nicknames that they had become a part of my identity through elementary school in San Francisco. But "goopeater" is not something any twelve-year-old boy wants to be associated with.

The insults usually started at lunch. Every day, I would arrive at the lunchroom trembling with fear. I and my khichdi, a concoction of lentils, vegetables and rice that Ma never failed to lovingly pack in my stainless steel lunchbox, would be humiliated. What nasty reaction would her love bring today?

Athena, the lunchroom bully, always made me cringe. On the face of it, she epitomised her name. Sure, she was the most beautiful girl in school, with big brown eyes, flowing black locks and a body so luscious that all the guys wanted to worship her. But, beneath the facade of a Greek goddess, she was nothing but a bully, every bit as fierce as The Boys in the schoolyard.

Athena never missed an opportunity to taunt me. Entering the lunchroom, she gracefully slithered into her usual seat at the far end of the table.

'Goop again?' she called. 'Sucks for you!'

I winced awkwardly and looked the other way. She was definitely more Medusa than Athena, and one day her mocking expression would turn me to stone. What had her parents been thinking when they named her? They probably hadn't been thinking at all.

'So, what's on the menu today?' she asked. 'Brown slimy goop or green smelly goop?'

Now, I was a huge fan of Ma's Ayurvedic cooking, I loved how she whipped up delicious dishes that were healthy at the same time. But goop? That was a label I could do without. Was this my punishment for showing up at school with Ma's nutrition-loaded lunches?

'Smelly goop givin' you a head rush?'

I clenched my fists, trying not to react, but it was tough to digest these insults, especially when they were hurled at you every single day. I recalled Ma's words—'A crusader cannot change the world if he allows himself to be vulnerable.' Uggh, it didn't make any sense, not in this context at least, so why did Ma keep repeating this to me? I didn't want to be a crusader!

'Get out of my face, Athena!' I screamed.

Then followed the head rush—hot blood spiralled up towards my head, turning my ears bright red as Athena carried on with her performance like an overenthusiastic cheerleader.

'Goopeater! Eater of goop! Eating stuff that looks like poop!'

And true to her routine, she reached for my food and smashed it against the wall. Laughter rippled through the lunchroom as soon as my so-called goop hit the wall. I could feel myself growing tinier than a first grader.

Delighted by her audience's response, Athena used a spoon to flick the kichdi in three different directions. I was puzzled and stared at my plate. The jarring sound of the label "goopeater" beat against the inside of my head amidst snorts and chuckles from other kids in the lunchroom.

Exiting the scene was the only available option. I gathered my empty, food-stained lunchbox and got up to leave the table. But Athena was always up for another challenge.

'Running for cover, are you?' she mocked.

That was it! By this time I was on a short leash, and the slightest remark was enough to set me off. Athena knew this all too well. I reached over to seize her chocolate pudding and splattered it all over her white shirt. It was almost a reflex action. Less than ten seconds later, I regretted my act.

Athena knew that Bick, the lunchroom monitor, would soften at the first sign of her damsel-in-distress tactics. She wailed, waved her arms and her massive trembling lips uttered, 'He's terrorising me!'

Bick was a burly old guy who was kind of slow in his reflexes, and more than a tad grumpy, maybe because he'd grown tired of this daily drama. He stormed over to the table, scowling at me with his hands on his hips. 'You *again*!' At that moment, I hated everything—Bick, Athena, kichdi, Ma! Oh, there was so much I wanted to say but what was the point? It never amounted to anything. Athena always managed to get away, thanks to her good looks and art of playing tricks. Besides, nobody ever believed a goopeater. So, I just stared sullenly at the floor.

'Make sure you stay behind and clean up this mess,' Bick said, 'even if it means missing the rest of lunch break.'

But you know what? His words meant nothing. Moments like these meant I would react. Instantly. It had become a conditioned reflex.

'You clean it up,' I growled in response. 'I'm outta here!'

And with that I headed for the door.

'You'd better freeze in your tracks,' Bick warned me, 'or I'll have the Head of the School after you.'

I knew that lunch duty would keep Bick busy in the cafeteria for at least another twenty minutes, so, why miss this chance? I grabbed my skateboard and stomped out of the lunchroom, towards the wall behind the dilapidated swings in the schoolyard.

The swing set was at the back of the yard. I was convinced that the other kids were not very fond of it because they didn't like the mural on the wall. I gazed at the brightly painted design that showed an African American kid, a Hispanic kid and a White kid playing together in harmony. The motto of Mckinley Middle School was "We Stand Together", but what kind of a message was that? I was the only South Asian kid at school. Not like there weren't other Asians around—the school had enough Chinese and Korean kids for sure—but I was different even to them. San Francisco is filled with Asians of all kinds but they all go to geek schools; Ma and Pa had insisted on McKinley because they wanted me to integrate. Yeah, sure, integration is all very well in theory but what was the point of it at a school where South Asians didn't feature in the mural representing racial harmony? I was an oddity and it was for this simple reason that the other school kids never hung out with me.

I spat at the wall and got up to find another place to spend the rest of the recess. But right then, I ran into the very last people I wanted to see that afternoon—The Boys.

My blood curdled at the sight of their smirking faces. You see, The Boys had a couple of years on me; they were known to be the coolest kids in school; but for me, they were harbingers of bad news. On the comparison scale, they made even Athena seem a harmless child. Elias was the most well-built of them all. His flaming red hair, big puffy cheeks and small squinty eyes were set atop a well-built body that you wouldn't want to be pitted against in a wrestling match.

He was their leader. His facade of friendliness disintegrated once he opened his mouth to expose a set of crooked teeth with wide gaps and stale food sticking out. It never failed to make me squirm. Behind him, stood his slovenly entourage: Jackson, a slanty-eyed kid with a thin build and bony fingers, a Giants baseball cap on his head and jacket worn back-to-front; Zak, a dishevelled looking kid, with torn khakis who smelled like he never showered; Alec, a dark-skinned dude, who, with his underwear sticking out of his jeans and almost reaching his hips, looked like he was straight out of a gangsta rap video; Jet and Mitch resembled evil twins from the projects donning black leather jackets and studded bracelets that would double up as power weapons during brawls.

The five of them rubbed their palms against each other at once. They stared at me menacingly, freezing me right to the very bone. Slowly, I flipped on to my skateboard and glided down a secluded path at the end of the yard.

'Hey, Arya Bin Laden!' Elias called. 'Where do you think you're going?'

For a second time that afternoon, I clenched my fists in an attempt to hold back. I wanted to ignore Elias's comments but I was edging towards the tipping point.

'What? Headin' home to goop-mama in the terror den?'

My pulse quickened at the shock of this new insult. First, a goopeater and then a terrorist. I could handle every snide remark, but why did they have to bring my mother into it too? It was one thing to be at the receiving end of a direct insult, but as far as I was concerned, nobody was allowed to attack my family. I wanted to hit Elias with my skateboard, instead I just stood there, trying to resist the urge to mouth obscenities.

'I smell something rotten!' Elias smirked. 'Uh oh everybody, goop for starters ends in farters!' He high-fived the others as they burst into laughter.

That was it. I couldn't control my anger any longer.

'Stop bothering me, Elias,' I said, my eyes on fire.

'Bothering you? Who's bothering who?'

'I'm not doing anything, I'm just hanging out in the schoolyard.'

'Yeah, but you're taking up our space!' Zak said, pushing me off and kicking my board into the wall.

'Go away!'

'*What'd you say?*'

I bit my lip recalling Ma's advice, 'Keeping quiet is better than speaking in anger.' I looked up as the four boys crowded around me.

'Arrr-yaaa insulting me?'

Damn my name! No matter where I went, I just couldn't escape it! Ma insisted that "Arya" was a privileged name, that belonged to India's ancient Sun Dynasty. It didn't bother me at home, but I'd grown to detest it during the school day, just like the goddamned khichdi! I glared at The Boys.

'You don't own the yard!'

'Yeah?' sneered Elias. 'Well, that's where you're wrong.'

And with a laugh that sent chills down my spine, Jet and Alec grabbed my backpack and smashed it against the fence. Zak pinned my arms to my back while Mitch tweaked my inflamed ears. Elias sniggered as he rested my skateboard at an angle up against the wall and then stamped through it, thrashing it to smithereens and Jackson just stood there jeering at the entire spectacle.

My beloved skateboard! I stared in horror at the remnants of this prized possession strewn all over the ground. Skating was the one thing I could do well. After months of pleading, Pa had finally given me the board on my last birthday—not too fancy or anything, but I treasured it above anything else. Riding it was my favourite thing to do.

When Zak turned to grin triumphantly at Elias, it took me a split second to kick him in the shins and wriggle free of his grip. Then, I took off. I sprinted towards the front of the yard. All the boys chased me. Other kids in the yard cheered at the spectacle like they were supporting a team of athletes on a track field. Problem was they were cheering for the other team.

My only option was to run out of the school gates to some other place where I didn't have to answer a bunch of bullies.

The louder they cheered, the faster I ran. Within moments, I outran all of them.

Then I heard a familiar voice. 'You can beat them, boy!'

It was Niklas, the school janitor. From the corner of my eye, I glanced at the white-haired old man who was the only other person as scrawny as me. Niklas's twinkling eyes added a sparkle to his wrinkled face. His age betrayed his stunning physique. His muscles stood out as though he were some poster child for a fitness magazine.

Why Niklas had a soft spot for me, I had no idea, I could hear his words echoing in my head, '*You can beat them, boy.*' Niklas knew that being scrawny had one crucial advantage: speed. My dark brown skin and jet black hair didn't get me places at McKinley Middle School but being the skinniest kid awarded me the title of the fastest runner in school. However, there was no time to deliberate. Just as I thought I had escaped, I bumped straight into the Head of the School.

'Arya,' he said, his arms crossed firmly. 'In my office, please. It appears that you and I need to have a chat.'

~

The Head's office was a dark, wood-panelled room, its walls adorned with more diplomas than I had seen in my mother's Ayurvedic health clinic. The wood had a distinct oaky smell laced with the faint aroma of coffee. An ashtray sat at the edge of a large leather inlaid desk.

I perched on the edge of a hardwood chair across from the Head, and couldn't help but notice his massive, hairy hands. They seemed inordinately large, too large perhaps, for a human being. In fact in many ways, the Head looked more like a big old ape than a man. He certainly had the body of a primate, the kind I'd taken care of in the San Francisco Zoo during a summer internship the previous year. His soft simian expression, flanked by a set of oversized spectacles was almost too friendly and a mismatch to his body structure.

'Yet another incident at lunch today?' the Head asked, cracking his big, hairy knuckles. 'When is this going to stop?'

'Wasn't my fault!' I replied, kicking the table. 'All they ever do is call me objectionable names like "goopeater" and "terrorist"'.

The Head swivelled in his chair, wondering how to be sympathetic and strict at the same time.

'I realise that your ethnic background can sometimes put you in a tough spot, but, you know, life is all about realising that what you see as an obstacle can actually be an asset!'

To be honest, all I could focus on were his massive, hairy hands. The Head's ring finger on his left hand was adorned with a solid gold ring.

'Arya, are you listening?' he asked.

I kicked my feet again.

'Do you think that reacting without thinking will help you achieve popularity?' He slapped his hand on the desk making a thud against the wood.

Popularity? What could he know about that? Being popular was the privilege of those kids who looked like they were part of a soft drink advertisement celebrating so-called diversity, with the white-skinned kids or very dark-brown ones, but without a place for anyone in-between. With words like "ethnic background" and "reacting without thinking", it made me wonder whether the Head and my mother had, somehow, planned their speeches to be in sync. And I was always the one who ended up in a mess.

'Are you even aware of what's happening in your school?' I asked. 'How come Athena and The Boys don't get into trouble?'

He looked at me with an expression that pierced my soul. 'Trouble comes in peaks and troughs, Arya. Those that cause it will bear the pain of punishment. But you experience a different kind of pain—one that is not well served by reaction. Remember, it's always reaction to a crime that incites violence, hardly ever the crime itself.'

'Great! So am I the criminal then?' I asked. 'Am I going to be in detention again?'

The Head sighed and swung around in his big leather chair. 'Arya, what good is detention when you obviously don't learn much from it?'

I shrugged, kicking my shoes against the desk.

The Head pursed his lips. 'There is no point in your staying here today. Why don't you take the afternoon off?'

I jumped upright. There was a math test scheduled for that afternoon.

'Are you suspending me? You can't,' I argued. 'Pa will be upset if I get an "F" just for being absent.' But the Head didn't seem concerned.

'I think that this situation is worth more of your time than your math test,' he replied. 'Go home and think about all this.'

'But...'

'No buts,' the Head said. 'Consider this *your education for today.*'

Culture Schmulture

Ma's work always kept her preoccupied. As an Ayurvedic doctor, she had slogged her way to successfully incorporating India's ancient system of medicine into San Francisco's public healthcare centres. However, she didn't have an easy time dealing with the bureaucracy of San Francisco's hospitals.

When she arrived home that day, the worry lines on her forehead appeared to be quite prominent, and she looked thinner than usual. This was accentuated by the fact that her shiny jet black hair was pulled back into a tight bun. I didn't know the cause of her distress, but, she looked old suddenly. It was puzzling—Ma had been blessed with a perfect complexion; her Ayurvedic diet kept her younger and fitter than anyone her age. But in the last few months, she'd started looking more worn out with each passing day.

Ma had a knack of being able to read me like a book. One look at me slurping canned spaghetti and she could sense trouble.

'What happened?' she asked, swinging her key chain rapidly, a telling sign of anxiety.

I didn't respond.

'Where did you get that horrible processed spaghetti?'

Still nothing.

'Was it the food again?' she asked. She threw her keys down on the kitchen table and began to twist her ring nervously around her finger instead.

Of course! It had always been about the food, but I wouldn't dare say it. If there was one thing I was aware of, it was the power of my words. Or rather, their effect on Ma. The last thing I wanted was to hurt her feelings by venting on her.

'Just pack me a sandwich or even some fruit, Ma; this khichdi is kind of embarrassing every day!' I tried my best to control the turmoil inside.

But Ma, obsessed with healthy cooking, wouldn't hear of shortcuts. It had to be a complete, balanced Ayurvedic meal.

'We're not the kind of family that feeds itself on processed food that has been stripped of its nutrients,' she responded.

'What's wrong with a sandwich?' I pleaded. 'I just want to fit in!'

Mother grimaced. 'I want you to fit in too, but I have a radically different idea about how a boy should establish his ethnic identity.'

Her red face was enough to tell me that she was getting angry.

'Life is not about sacrificing your culture of wellness just to fit in,' she said. Her voice betrayed undertones of exasperation. I could see from her facial expression that she was making an effort to stay calm.

'I give you pure, unadulterated food of the gods. It empowers you to battle the demons of everyday life.'

'What demons? I'm not a character from the Ramayana!'

'The demons of ill health, Arya. Digestive weakness, low immunity and a toxic mind. These work against the building blocks of strength that you must nourish in order to take on just about everything else that comes your way.'

It wasn't that I hated Ayurvedic food. In fact, I devoured each of Ma's meals with relish at home. But school was a different story. I couldn't stand the label that had become part of my lunchtime identity and she just didn't get it!

'Your body is composed of rasa, the very essence of the food that you eat,' she explained. 'Food is the building block of life, and ours is the building block of our culture as well.'

Ma would never understand that khichdi was goop, or that goop was the building block of unpleasant lunchtime experiences! Everything about it was gross. Its yellow-brown, unappealing look and texture underscored my own unacceptability in the face of others. As a goopeater, I could never be part of the in-group. On most days, Athena's harassment ended with my lunch being thrown across the table, but today I had lost my skateboard too, the one thing that could actually earn me some respect was gone. It was a no-win situation.

'Culture schmulture,' I said scowling. It was a knee-jerk reaction. Like I said, deep down I didn't want to hurt her, but some devil inside urged me to intentionally use words that I knew would torment her.

Torn between anger and despair, Ma decided to call it quits for the evening.

'Say your prayers and go to bed, IMMEDIATELY!' she said.

'But what about Prince Rama?'

Mother's post-dinner prayer ritual had always been the highlight of my day. Never once did I tire of listening to her narrate the antics of Rama, the prince of Ayodhya and hero of India's ancient epic, the Ramayana. His battles against Ravana, the demon king of Lanka, and his entourage of demons—they always put into context my own struggles. I might have been close to thirteen, but as far as I was concerned, I'd never be too old for the stories.

'No stories for you tonight,' she said in a carefully controlled tone.

I looked at her weakly.

'But Ma...'

'What part of "no" do you not understand Arya?'

Obviously, she meant business. Sulking, I shuffled down the corridor towards my room.

~

Ma always told me that my biggest weakness is that I am hypersensitive, that I react instantly and tend to take things too easily to heart. Pa said it was something that I should have grown out of long ago, and you know what? I tried. But how do you change something that's been part of your personality from the get-go? When I got upset, it was like some greater power would take control of my emotions making me want to react instantly by hitting or spitting or turning on the taps. Turning on the taps—that was the worst. I was too old to cry but it was something that almost always happened at home and when it did, I just couldn't control it.

As Ma sat meditating in her prayer room, I tried my best to muffle the sounds of my uncontrollable sobbing under the comforter.

But she must have sensed that I was upset. She knew that even though I hadn't explicitly shared the details of my day, something terrible had happened. She made her way over to her usual spot by my bed and began to gently stroke my hair.

'Ravana, the ten-headed demon king of Lanka, advanced towards Rama, spitting fire into each tree he trampled down on the way.'

I looked up and my eyes met Ma's smiling face. How did she know these stories were my elixir? At that moment, she was the most beautiful angel imaginable.

'Rama stayed calm as he stood there anticipating the demon king's approach, his bow strung to his arrow. No threat of danger could ruffle the prince's feathers; he knew the slightest agitation would ruin his focus.'

I pictured myself in the prince's place, fighting the bullies in the schoolyard. And each time, they would give me a better understanding of Rama's warrior discipline. How could Rama stay calm in the face of constant evil, I had no idea, but his battles against the demons grew increasingly vivid in my mind.

That evening, the stories were especially illuminating. I was enraptured by Rama's victory against Ravana. The fact that Rama had nothing but a bow, an arrow, and an army of monkey-people called vanaras, made me admire him even more.

As Ma described each martial technique with extreme precision, I imagined myself single-handedly fighting Elias and The Boys, just as Rama had fought Ravana and his army of demons.

'The crouch-before-leaping method intensified the impact, giving Rama the ability to leap at his target like a tiger at its prey,' Ma continued. 'The rakshasas, the demons that is, used swords, shields, flexible knives and poisoned arrows to set fire to their targets immediately upon contact,' explained Ma.

How could a woman possess knowledge about the functions and magical effects of weapons?

'The Arya race was a group of brave crusaders, who existed to protect themselves and their kin from evil. Both men and women were equipped with knowledge of martial arts. Besides, they were given a different kind of handcrafted weapon made from the simplest of elements but used with utmost skill,' she said.

Visions of weapons raced across my mind. I would have been better equipped to deal with trouble from The Boys, had I known how to access them.

'Remember, weapons work only when they are used with the right intention,' she continued. 'If your intentions are wrong, then your efforts will only lead to further torment.'

What did she mean by that?

Ma laughed as though she could read my mind. 'Always remember, your truest weapons are your humility and pride for your culture.'

I winced at the mention of the word "culture." Lately, it seemed to cause nothing but trouble.

'Retaining your culture in a foreign land is not an easy task,' Ma explained. 'But think of Rama, he too was faced with trouble, yet he kept his head held high. It is for this distinct quality that you were named Arya Vir, meaning the Brave Protector of the People.'

Sure, the name again! How could it possibly solve my problems when it always seemed to be their cause?

'Rama was the Brave Protector of the People too. Except for humility, he had nothing on his side. His weapons were powered by divine mantras—verses ordained by the gods.'

Divine mantras. My head pulsated. To think that a weapon could be "mantra-ised" to attain divine power, seemed fascinating. Did the gods descend from the heaven as warriors too?

'You could say,' Ma laughed again. 'The gods, after all, have a knack for showing up on earth when life goes so awry and we need them the most. It has happened over and over again.'

I felt the magnetic pull of sleep drawing me into its cocoon. Ma's voice drifted off...somewhere into my subconsciousness, 'We used to live in simpler times, closer to the gods than we are today; alongside vanaras, who have long since retreated deep into the forests.'

~

My dreams exploded with intricate scenes of Rama's exploits against the evil rakshasas of ancient India. As an archetype of the Aryas, I saw myself as a soldier in Rama's army, fighting heroically against the monstrous demons that harassed the peaceful forest dwellers. I saw myself battling against Ravana, alongside Rama's army of vanaras under the sturdy direction of their chieftain, Hanumana.

But then, a tap-tapping at my window interrupted it all.

'Arr-yaa!' cried out a familiar voice.

My blood froze as I sat upright to the ugly sound of Elias. Hadn't there been enough trouble for one day? I leapt out of my bed and pulled open the window with a firm resolve to take care of the situation once and for all.

'What do you want, Elias?'

But contrary to my expectation, he flashed me a smile, his ugly yellow teeth gleaming in the pale lamplight. I looked around in trepidation for the rest of the entourage.

'Relax dude,' Elias said. 'I just wanted to high-five you. That was supreme—how you skipped out on a math test!'

I was confused. Skipping the math test meant I had failed. Were they actually happy with that or was this really some kind of back-handed compliment? Then, I heard Ma's voice from the hallway. 'Arya? What's the matter?'

'Nothing Ma, go to sleep!' I replied, quickly turning back to the window. 'What do you want Elias?'

'Show up at Jackson's house for the Halloween party tomorrow,' Elias replied. 'The tricks'll be the treat.'

I couldn't believe my ears. An invitation to Jackson's Halloween party? Could it be true? I had never been invited before.

Before I could say anything else, Elias jumped on to his bike, and sped away. Soon Ma showed up next to me at the window.

'Who was that?' she asked, tying her belt around her housecoat, agitated.

'Just a friend.'

'A friend? At this hour? Why?'

'He was talking about a Halloween party,' I said, a smile slowly stretching across my face as I pictured the festivities.

'What's his name?' Ma asked suspiciously.

'Elias.'

'Elias?' she repeated. 'He's not your friend! That boy is up to no good.'

'Yeah well, he's good enough for me,' I replied with renewed ambition. It was best not to say too much. Still, Ma wasn't satisfied.

'Arya, what exactly happened today? Are you in some kind of trouble?'

Trouble? Not nearly enough. The thing was that trouble is just a state of mind, and sometimes exactly what you needed to get an invitation. It occurred to me that my quest for ways to get into trouble had just begun!

D-A-N-G-E-R

I arrived at Jackson's home the next day to find the front door wide open. The housekeeper stood on the porch handing out candy from a large earthenware pot to trick-or-treaters stopping by.

'Hello Arya,' she said smiling warmly. I looked at her suspiciously. How did she know my name? It wasn't like I'd been invited here before!

I stood there at the steps, hesitant to cross the threshold.

'Is Jackson here?' I asked.

'He's around the corner,' she replied.

A voice called out from inside the house. 'Adriana, who is it?'

Two women, dressed as witches, emerged from behind the door. The shorter, plump Good Witch in a blue sparkly dress grinned and glided towards me waving a lollipop wand in my face, but the other Bad Witch dressed in stark black kept her distance. Her bony face sat atop a long, thin neck poking out of a high-collared cloak emblazoned with stars and moons. It was Jackson's mother, I recognised her from the class open house the week before.

'It's Arya,' Adriana replied. 'The Indian boy.'

From her description, it was obvious that Adriana was aware of what had been going on.

'Oh!' Jackson's mother's voice dropped as she disapprovingly eyed me in my long black cloak with a black hood. I clutched my devil's mask tightly.

'Do you detect some curry munching?' she whispered, cocking her head over towards the Good Witch. 'These people are so awkward in their interaction with our boys.'

The Good Witch nodded, somewhat expressionless.

Uggh! Elias had invited me to the party! What the heck was Jackson's mother being mean to me for? This was supposed to be a good day.

I stood there awkwardly, scowling at the floor but luckily, Adriana saved the situation.

'Go on now, they are waiting for you,' she said stepping forward to usher me in the direction of the garden gate.

'Thank you,' I said trying to pull a half-smile. Then, guided by her, I slipped around the corner to find them.

The Boys had been waiting but little did I know what had they been waiting for. Initiation into a brotherhood meant executing a plan for ghoulish entertainment.

'Put on your mask,' Elias said. 'There's a golden statue of some guy in Jackson's mom's bedroom upstairs. It ain't too big, but it's old as shit. Now, think about the cash we could get if we sold that thing.'

'What does this have to do with me?' I asked, confused.

Elias flashed his ugly yellow teeth at me. 'Heck, you're gonna bring it to us!'

Me? Steal something? I was stumped. My parents would be livid if they knew.

'Like I said, there's a lotta cool stuff that can be bought with the cash,' Elias said, raising his eyebrow slyly, while the others sniggered in the background.

It didn't make sense, why wouldn't Jackson steal it himself?

'What's in it for me?' I asked, still suspicious.

'Dude, we know you can risk getting into trouble, but if you want to be one of us, you gotta show that you are ready to take those risks for us... and win. Are you cool enough to join The Boys or what?' Elias replied.

It was then clear as crystal. The task at hand was one that none of them wanted to risk, so, they had turned it over to me. Should I look at this as yet another taunt? Or as a golden opportunity to earn their respect?

'What if I fail?' I asked cautiously.

Elias sensed I was in two minds.

'Like I said, do you want in or what?' he insisted.

Of course, I did! It had to be done, there was no other way to win their respect!

'I'm on it,' I said, gritting my teeth.

I scanned the scene to plan my mission, put on my mask and followed them back to the front of the house. Jackson's father was standing at the front door, handing out a bunch of candy to the group of kids clustered around him. Soon after, he disappeared inside the kitchen to get another glass of wine.

'Go on then, now's your chance,' Alec hissed, pointing to the staircase.

I nodded, planning my mission silently.

'Go on, get up there and do it!' Alec urged. 'Up the stairs and first left on the landing.'

'Which door exactly? What if there is someone there?' I whispered back.

'Dude, there's no time for questions!' Alec said, turning his head to survey the scene. 'Now, are you doing this or are you gonna wimp out?'

'Wimp?' That was all I needed to hear to get riled up again. Without further ado, I dashed up the stairs and took an immediate left into what I thought was Jackson's parents' bedroom. I removed my mask for better night vision, but still it wasn't so easy. As I groped for signs of the statue in the dark, I accidentally tripped over something. Next, there was a thunderous clang, and I knew something large and obviously unstable had come crashing down. But, before I could tell what it was, Jackson's mother had burst into the room. She switched on the lights, took one look at me and let out a bloodcurdling scream.

'STALKER! I HAVE A STALKER! THE CURRY MUNCHING CREEP!'

I stood in shock as another racist insult hit me in the face and even though I wanted to attack her with equally racial slurs, for once, better judgement prevailed. With the nimbleness of a cat, I slipped on the mask again, brushed passed her out the door, jumped onto the bannister and slid all the way down to the first floor barely colliding with a new group of trick-or-treaters that had made its way into the foyer. I pushed past the crowds at the doorstep and sprinted out into the night.

~

Ma was completely beside herself the next day when Adriana showed up at our doorstep. She had been sent by Jackson's mother to question the events of the night before.

'My son? A stalker? That's impossible, these are not our values!' she insisted, distressed.

Adriana looked empathetic, as if she was in two minds herself.

'I know how you feel, my madam can get upset quite easily sometimes, especially when it comes to people like us,' she said.

Ma looked at her quizzically. 'What do you mean like us?'

'People of colour,' Adriana explained looking forlornly at the floor. 'But still, values are important. I don't know why he was in my madam's bedroom; thank the Lord that whatever he was doing didn't turn out to be anything more than simple trespassing.'

But thanking the Lord was the furthest thing from my mind. A failed attempt at robbery meant that my all-important attempt at gaining popularity with The Boys had been thwarted.

~

After that, life went back to square one.

'Dumbass!' Eliot called out in the schoolyard.

Great. From goopeater to terrorist to dumbass!

'I ain't no dumbass!' I retorted.

'Right, you're no dumbass, you're a dumbass loser who's good for eating goop, but not for stealing something that we could have sold for real M-O-N-E-Y!'

I stood back as Elias and The Boys sniggered at me from beyond the mural wall. Up until now, I'd been convinced that they had set a trap at Jackson's Halloween party, but now it became clear that The Boys actually did want the statue for themselves. Surely the other kids knew what these guys were made of. So why the heck were they such sychophants of The Boys—guys who steal!

Popularity! What a strange and ironic thing, belonging to bad people who did bad things. But I felt compelled to do those bad things too because it was the only way to look good in the eyes of others. Even if it meant hating what I stood for, it was the only way to get popular with those who mattered to everyone else. How else could a crusader ever build a following?

So, I spoke confidently.

'I CAN steal!'

'You need balls goopster,' Elias replied.

'I HAVE balls!' I said.

'Yeah, as much as girls do!'

The Boys chuckled loudly as Elias gave Alec a high five.

I was seething. The audacity of those guys—comparing me to a girl! As I walked home, I was focused on one idea—I had to steal something to prove myself to The Boys. So lost was I in my thoughts that it didn't occur to me to wait till the light had turned green before I could cross the road. A car scraped by, missing me by inches.

'What's wrong with you?' the driver yelled. 'You could have been killed!'

Yeah well, perhaps then I should have been killed. There had to be something better in the land beyond this living hell. I gaped at my reflection in the window of Amoeba Records, averting the crowd of people jostling by. Then, I had a light-bulb moment.

Nothing would work for me until I won the respect of The Boys. But to do that, I had to prove my self-worth. God had answered my prayers by bringing me to Amoeba Records, the historic record shop on San Francisco's famous Haight Street. It must be in my destiny to steal a CD!

I pushed through the front door and made my way to the aisle all the way at the back of the store where fewer people lurked. I browsed through all the selections—rock-and-roll, jazz, opera—but, with no interest in any particular genre or style. Then I picked up a CD and looked closely at its plastic case that reflected the neon light from the ceiling. A quick glance from the corner of my eye ascertained that the coast was clear but just as I was about to slip it under my jacket, I heard a voice, 'Caught you!'

I froze on the spot. A salesman peeped over at me from across the next aisle.

Dang it! Why did I always have the worst luck in the world? But the salesman had an excited grin on his face. And, his eyes seemed to change colour in the neon light. I instantly recognised the skinny figure of Niklas, the school janitor.

'I finally caught a kid who is interested in opera. Today is my lucky day!' he said. I looked down at the CD in my hands to see a copy of Carmen, sung by Pavarotti.

'That's probably one of the best versions of Carmen out there. Do you know he actually sang it here in San Francisco's symphony hall?'

I nodded my head emulating the eagerness of a student hungry for knowledge. Soon, he launched into a five-minute lecture about the wonders of sopranos, altos and other operatic terms that meant who-knows-what. Seeing it as an opportunity to plan my next move, I pretended to be completely enraptured.

'Niklas, can you help me with something?' I asked when the salesman paused for breath.

'Anything at all, boy.'

Boy! I looked closely into his eyes as his eyes appeared to change colour again.

'Since when do you work here by the way?' I asked.

'Hey, we've all got jobs. My job is to help folks like you,' he said. I thought quickly about how to take advantage of the situation.

'There's this specific piece of music that I am looking for,' I said. 'I can't remember the name but it combines an Italian opera with classical Indian music. I saw it in the World Music section the last time I came here, but I can't find it now.'

'Well, let's see if I can find it for you,' Niklas said, turning around to walk over to another part of the store. 'I'll be right back.' He winked at me and turned to walk away.

No sooner had he vanished from sight, than I slipped the Carmen CD under my jacket and made a dash for the front door. The bar code detector started to beep crazily as I approached the exit, but I sprinted down the street before anyone could figure out that I was the culprit.

Ten minutes later, I slowed my pace to catch my breath. I looked around. There was no one chasing after me—no cops, no angry salesmen. I heaved a sigh of relief and took out the CD from my jacket. Success! How cool was it that the janitor should be manning the music shop that day?

Why he had a soft spot for me, I did not have any idea. In my mind, Niklas was an accomplice to my crime. He'd never spill the beans, he understood that I needed to fit in. His words were especially profound—*My job is to help folks like you.* Yes indeed, I needed all the help I could get.

~

Flaunting my stolen treasure, still sealed in its protective plastic cover, earned me new respect from The Boys. None of them cared what CD it was, they just appreciated the fact that I'd stolen something from San Francisco's most famous record shop. I'd nailed it! I had proven my worth—I was no dumbass.

After that, things really changed. My successful theft convinced The Boys of my level of commitment to their cause. I was now part of their gang, as long as I was willing to dabble with trouble. Like them.

'Dude, you gotta down this,' Elias said at the park one Sunday, shoving a shot of some nasty-smelling alcohol under my nose.

I hesitated, staring at the liquid through the mouth of the bottle. I knew it spelled D-A-N-G-E-R.

'C'mon,' Elias coaxed. 'Time to get fired up for our race down MLK.'

MLK was the road that wound its way around the entire stretch of the park. Like the Amoeba Records episode, here was another opportunity. The Boys knew I was the fastest skater in town. It was perhaps the main reason why they had accepted me into their group. Without me, they'd have to work really hard to win all the park races, but with me they stood no chance of losing. Deep down I knew they were using me but hey, at last I was part of the cool gang.

Alec presented me with his own skateboard as a mark of respect for being initiated into the group.

'Sorry we broke yours, buddy,' he said. 'But ya know, a guy's gotta do what a guy's gotta do! Here, take mine; it makes for an awesome ride after a couple of tequila shots.'

I pushed away all thoughts about what would happen should Ma find out; acceptance meant playing according to the rules. Their rules, not mine and definitely not those of my parents.

Elias's voice broke my train of thought. 'Dude, are you chickening out?'

That was all the coaxing I needed. I swiped the bottle out of his hands and chugged down the nasty-tasting liquid.

Skateboarding down MLK after drinking was like fleeing from a band of fire-spitting rakshasas in a dream sequence. I felt like a feather floating through the breeze. I recklessly swerved through a sea of people, strollers and bicycles, till I crashed into a thorny rose bush at the entrance of the Botanical Gardens. My skin ripped in a million places and my left side was in deep pain. I don't even want to think about what could have happened to my skull were it not for the helmet on my head.

I staggered home that afternoon, bruised, blood-stained and just short of swooning from the effects of alcohol, which couldn't lessen the pain of my injuries. Pa wasn't around when I got there. Ma's face fell when she took one look at my sprained arm. Then, she caught a whiff of alcohol.

I knew exactly what she was thinking. She couldn't believe that the son she had worked so hard to bring up with good Vedic values had let her down again! I looked sheepishly in another direction.

'Alcohol?!'

'I don't wanna talk about it,' I replied, my face shrunk to the size of a mouse.

'Arya, I'm your mother, I need to know!'

'Leave me alone! You don't need to know anything,' I screamed, partly in irritation and partly from the pain of my sprained arm.

She drove me to the emergency room with the speed of a bullet train. I kept my mouth shut throughout the next two hours, speaking only when the doctor asked specific questions.

When we returned home, Ma tried to lure me with her gourmet Ayurvedic cooking, but I didn't want any. I just wanted to be left alone, so I disappeared into my room and slammed the door shut.

~

Once my wounds had healed, it became easier to hide the subsequent episodes from my parents. It's not like I had a choice—Ma would never understand what it took to be popular and Pa had little time to spare from driving his taxi around town. So, they had no idea that I hung out on the corner, smoking cigarette butts collected from the sidewalks of rotten neighbourhoods. They didn't know about the day I had narrowly escaped being caught shoplifting for the second time at Amoeba Records, when the gang dared me repeat my act.

But Ma could smell trouble from miles away.

'Arya, what kind of a friend wants to be friendly, as long as you are willing to walk a dangerous path, solely for his entertainment? Would Rama do it?' she asked one day. Rama again! Sure, he'd never cross over to the side of evil, but he didn't have to deal with the trauma of an interfering mother each day. I ignored her, because in my mind, she'd become a nuisance.

'It's the best way to deal with parents who constantly butt into your life,' Jackson had said. He should know considering his zero respect policy that made him ask me to steal something from his own mother's room at Halloween! At first it was weird hiding things from Ma but over time it became easier. Soon, telling lies became a habit.

Still amidst all this, the one thing I couldn't let go of was her stories. Like magic, they would draw me back to her each evening. And every time she recounted the tales of the vanaras, it was like she zapped away my anger and turned me to a little boy once again.

Rite of Passage

'Arya is almost thirteen,' Ma told Pa over brunch one day. 'It's time we had his thread ceremony.'

My thread ceremony? Was she for real? It was an age-old custom in which Brahmin boys were formally inducted into the learnings of India's ancient Vedic texts. This ceremony must have been a good idea perhaps, in the days when learning was synonymous to the Vedas. People did nothing of that sort these days. Not many studied the Vedas today and even those who did, became pandits visiting different homes to perform religious rites.

Uh uh! I didn't need any kind of public induction into anything religious.

'A thread ceremony is nothing but an excuse to have a coming-out party,' I said, my brow completely knotted.

'Do you really think so?' Pa asked, taken aback. He seemed to have lost weight probably because he was worried about finances and the economy. The anxiety never did him any good—his wiry frame, silver grey hair and lean bone structure made him look gaunt as he grew older and more anxiety-ridden.

But Ma was quick to interject, 'I don't believe you have a problem with coming-out parties. I think, as far as you are concerned, you've already had yours. No?'

Quite right. My moment of transformation had already taken place the day The Boys accepted me as "cool". A few months ago, when Ma's words had sounded like music to my ears, the mention of a thread ceremony might not have posed a problem. But then, the very mention of the Vedas or anything to do with Hinduism brought back that deep-seated feeling of "different-ness" I had taken so long to overcome.

'Don't impose the culture thing!' I said, scraping the butter knife on the surface of the table. Couldn't they see I was frustrated?

'I'm not imposing anything!' Ma replied, equally irritated. 'This is a chance to invite your friends to become a part of who you really are!'

Great! Now, friends were part of this stupid plan too? I dug my nails into my fists and looked at Pa pointedly.

'What do my friends have to do with this?'

But Pa simply shrugged his shoulders, handing the reins over to his wife.

'It's been fifteen years since your Pa and I left India,' she said. 'Our community is no longer a narrow section of Indians living in a foreign land, but a wider group that includes our colleagues and friends in San Francisco, the families we meet at the temple and the families that are part of your school.'

'Nobody in my school is like *us*!' I said. I could feel my nails piercing through the outer skin on my palms. Ma sighed.

'Arya, I know it hasn't been easy, but, we have made sacrifices to put you in this school. We thought it would be best for your education. Your classmates are now part of our extended community.'

'But they're not!' By now I was completely exasperated. 'They're different. They don't live the way we brown folks do!'

'It doesn't matter,' Ma said stubbornly. 'Community attendance is very important in the Vedic rites of passage.'

What utter crap! Could Ma really be so naive as to think that my friends would be into anything Vedic?

'My friends don't know the first thing about this stuff.'

'Which is why this is a wonderful opportunity for them to learn. It is their right. The words "right" and "rite" come from "Rita", the cosmic law of morality defined by the Vedas.'

'Nobody cares about rights, rites or Vedas!' I yelled. I flung the butter knife across the table. Ma pursed her lips, trying to maintain her composure.

She turned to Pa who folded away his newspaper and cleared his throat.

'Arya, don't you think your Ma knows best about these things?' he asked.

I adored my parents but when they said stuff that pissed me off, I had a hard time controlling my mean streak.

'Yeah? Is that why YOU never have anything to say around here?' I barked.

Truth is, I couldn't stand his absence so I used it as a reason to taunt him.

'Arya, don't talk to your father like that!' Ma shouted.

'It's alright,' Pa said, clearly a little taken aback. 'Perhaps he has a point.'

He took off his glasses and leaned over towards me.

'Now listen, I know you think that I am not by your side all the time during your growing up years, but the truth is,

I am. It's just that your mother is the more seasoned parent when it comes to imparting Hindu values.'

'Frankly, you don't really care whether I'm good or bad. You have no idea what I do.' Pa gaped at me, dumbfounded.

'Is that what this is all about?' Ma asked in shock, 'Do you really think that your father doesn't care?'

'As much as terrorists care about world peace. And besides, what's all this crap about earning a living. You're just a cab driver.'

'Enough!' Ma begged. 'You have to break this habit of overreacting!'

I chewed on the end of my napkin and then spat. Seeing Ma put her head in her hands, Pa tried to salvage the conversation.

'Arya, so what if your Ma wants to have a thread ceremony? The Jewish kids have Bar Mitzvahs and the Catholics look forward to their First Holy Communion...'

'I ain't Jewish and I don't give a hang about Holy Communions!'

'That's someone's religion you are disrespecting!' Pa retorted.

'Why should I care? It's not like anyone else happens to respect mine!'

The conversation was going nowhere. Without further ado, I got up and ran outside.

But as soon as I'd crossed the front yard, I realised that The Boys were actually the last people I wanted to see that afternoon. All I needed was some time alone; I needed to figure out how to get the thread ceremony idea out of Ma's head. Elias could probably advise me best, but I wasn't ready to risk blurting out anything about a Vedic rite of passage. They'd just about stopped calling me a terrorist.

That afternoon, I remember climbing hill after hill in San Francisco. I walked all the way to the eastern side of the city. As I approached Chinatown, I saw a series of freshly painted graffiti murals on the wall of Rainbow grocery store, the local supermarket. Unlike gang marks and scribbles that vandalise public property, I saw that an artist had created this, probably commissioned by the store. It was a picture of a beautiful forest landscape filled with waterfalls and rainbows in different shapes. The colours and brushstrokes breathed life into the painting. It felt like I was standing at the edge of heaven.

I scoured the wall, thinking about the dual characteristics of the graffiti. Sometimes, it was considered an art form yet at other times, it symbolised a defacement of public property. It reminded me of the mural on the wall at school. If it was supposed to depict racial harmony then why didn't it include any brown people? Suddenly, at the bottom right corner of the wall, my eye caught a piece of shining silver metal. It was a can of red spray paint left behind by the graffiti artist.

Impulse took over my moral self. I snatched up the can and sprayed big, red circles all over the bottom part of the wall until the paintings were barely visible any more. Then, staring gleefully at my wrongdoing, I calmly walked inside the store to tell the owner about it.

The store owner rushed out in a frenzy to examine the damage. He took one look at the wall and wailed loudly.

He couldn't understand why I was so calm as he shouted out to his customers about what had happened.

'You vandalise my property and then turn yourself in? I don't understand it!'

I had once read in some magazine that petty criminals sometimes turn themselves in after performing acts of destruction as a way to reconcile themselves with the evil actions of their past. Little did I know then that I was actually reconciling myself with my future.

The World Turned Upside Down

When Ma arrived at the store after receiving a frantic call from its owner, she was devastated. She was distressed by not only the damage I had done, or the amount due in damages but what had really got her upset was my smug response. Like a seasoned criminal, I had no remorse.

As soon as we began to walk home, she got straight to the point.

'Why Arya?' she asked. 'Why this senseless act? Why is it such a victory for you?'

I looked at the stones of the sidewalk. Truth be told, I didn't feel so victorious anymore, but I didn't outwardly change my stance.

''Cos…' I replied, kicking my feet into the ground as I walked.

I clasped my hands comfortably behind my neck to try and show her that I couldn't care less.

'You did this to embarrass us, didn't you?' Ma asked.

'Not like you don't do enough to embarrass me,' I retorted.

She took a deep breath and tilted her head to one side. 'So, you assumed that by doing this, you could, what, get even?'

'Maybe,'

'About what?'

I stopped in my tracks, arms crossed. 'I don't want a thread ceremony!' I barked.

'I see,' she said without prolonging the discussion.

As we walked passed the shops on the way home, Ma stared into the distance without really looking. Her fixed, expressionless eyes resembled the glass eyes of a doll. Very unusual for her. Ma didn't say anything else for a long time after that. So I decided to broach the topic.

'So, it's off?'

She glanced at me, surprised.

'Excuse me?'

'Now that you have all the damage money to pay and you hate me, I assume we'll cancel the party.'

Ma's face slowly broke into a careful smile with renewed determination.

'Arya, even your most foolhardy behaviour cannot stop me from loving you enough to give you what you need.'

'Huh?' I said, confused.

'I don't hate you, and you *will* have your thread ceremony.'

'But ...'

'You need to understand the value of the Vedas more than I had realised.'

Instantly, I turned red in the face.

'No friggin' way!'

Leaving her on the sidewalk, I ran across the road in the midst of a noisy rush-hour traffic. Two cars and a bus swerved to avoid me as I sprinted to the other side. Although the cars managed to screech without causing too much damage, the bus was not so lucky.

At that precise moment, the bus driver took a sudden curve to avoid hitting me but lost control. The massive vehicle spun its wheels, detached from its gripping cables and slid headlong into the sidewalk where Ma stood petrified.

I looked around but it was too late—the left side of her body had been crushed by the bus's rear-wheel as it hurtled down the hills of Chinatown.

~

The next few moments were a nightmarish whirlwind flowing through my subconscious mind. I could barely make sense of what had happened. A large crowd gathered over Ma and within moments an ambulance arrived on the scene. Two paramedic workers strapped her on to a stretcher and rushed her to the nearest emergency room.

I was in a complete daze. People swarmed around me and within moments, I was flooded with questions.

'Are you alright?'

'Did you sec the bus coming?'

'Why did you run across the road?'

But I didn't know the answers. I just stood there, shell-shocked as the noise around me rose to an incomprehensible din. It was like I was watching a silent movie.

~

A barrage of questions later, two policemen escorted me to my worry-stricken father, who had been summoned home in the middle of his afternoon shift. He sank to the floor speechless, like he had seen a ghost.

By the time we arrived at the hospital, Ma was already strapped to a life-support machine.

'She's in a coma,' the doctor said, without a trace of emotion. 'If she doesn't come out of it in the next forty-eight hours, it is not clear that she ever will.'

I could hardly believe my ears. *A coma that had come out of an accident that had come out of a quarrel.* I tried my best to rationalise the situation—she was in coma because of me, yet I had escaped, unscathed. Pa's face turned ashen. My heart was stung by the bitterness of regret.

We didn't make it home that night. Or to school, or work the next day. For two whole days, I sat glued to a hard hospital chair in Ma's room, while Pa paced the halls outside. How did our world turn upside-down in a matter of moments, and that too without any warning?

The Fault Line

Three weeks later, nothing had changed.

The hospital staff got tired of nursing Ma day after day in one of their coveted rooms.

'I'm sorry to tell you this,' the doctor said, his pristine white coat reeking of spray starch, 'but she's showing no signs of improvement.'

Pa responded with a blank look. He didn't register what the doctor was trying to suggest. So the doctor tried again.

'You might want to consider taking her off the life support,' he snapped.

The words struck me like a burning arrow. Disconnecting mother's life-support systems would mean disconnecting her from life itself. How could a doctor, of all people, be inhuman enough to suggest this?

But for this particular one, it was obviously just another day on the job.

I was consumed by a sudden hatred for him. 'It doesn't make any sense,' I said stamping my foot fiercely. Like that was going to make any difference.

'My mother is a doctor too. An Ayurvedic doctor! But unlike you, she's supposed to help sick people, not turn them away or become one of them herself.'

I clenched my fists tight as hot blood rushed to my ears turning them bright red.

Pa had now become hysterical.

'She has a child, a husband! We're her family,' he yelled.

Wow! Pa was always so calm. I'd never seen him lose it.

'I understand that this is hard for you,' the doctor croaked looking at the time on his watch. He also glanced through the notes on a clipboard. 'But we need the hospital beds for those we *can* truly help.'

'*Can* or *will*?' Pa retorted. 'Does my wife's life hold less value than that of others?'

The doctor rolled his eyes. 'That's not what I'm trying to say.'

'What *are* you trying to say?' Pa shouted. 'That we are poor? Coloured? Foreign? Or is it that we do not speak as well as you do?'

Pa's seething rage astounded me. He had always seemed quiet, unperturbed and almost uncaring—quite unlike the firebrand who was now rebuking the medical man in white coat.

However, nothing seemed to affect the doctor. He just walked away.

~

After a day of intense negotiation, Pa and the doctor reached a compromise. They'd move Ma to a nursing home outside the city, where she would not "bother" anyone, as long as he continued to pay her medical bills.

I hated the thought but what could I do?

'It's dust under the rug, isn't it?' I asked.

Pa nodded his head without saying a word.

The accident marked the end of life as I knew it. I'd gone from having a spirited mother who had always been the fulcrum of stability and joy in my life, to having a lifeless remnant of one instead.

Give it time, the nursing home staff advised, but there was no telling how much time was required to bring back her laughter. The scent of her Ayurvedic oils still wafted down the corridors, filling our home with the aroma of loneliness.

~

At school, things became unbearable once again. Thoughts of Ma kept me distracted, leaving little time to think about The Boys. However, when they showed up, they were completely unsympathetic. But I didn't feel like dancing to their tune anymore.

The relationship I had worked so hard to build with The Boys crumbled like chalk. Perhaps I had failed to meet their expectations and risky challenges.

In a matter of days, I went back to being a goopeater. Soon after, a terrorist.

Every new day meant a new round of clashes. The Headmaster simply shook his head and pounded his desk with his hairy knuckles.

'Why not derive strength rather than anger from your mother's condition?' he asked.

But his words made no sense. How do you derive strength from a comatose being? I wanted to save her but I also hated her for what she had become. I resolved never to return to the nursing home.

~

But even in the midst of this hopeless atmosphere, an interesting development took shape at home. Pa's presence suddenly filled the vacuum that Ma's absence had left behind. He altered his work shifts to greet me every afternoon when I got back home from school. He started doing things that I hadn't really seen him do before. Like cooking. He made fragrant curries and slow-cooked dal—the kind of sumptuous delicacies that had been Ma's forte. He drove me to school and supervised my homework, teaching me math tricks that he'd learned as a boy in his village school. Maybe it was a deliberate effort to stay busy, to distract himself so that he didn't turn into a puddle in my presence. But I felt that Pa had acquired a whole new set of skills overnight. I wasn't particularly talkative those days so I wouldn't really comment, but I definitely developed a newfound respect for my old man.

The one big gaping hole in my life was the absence of Ma's prayer ritual followed by the Ramayana stories. Pa didn't have the skill to describe Rama's battle scenes or relate the travails of the vanaras with the same eye for detail. So, he didn't even try to compensate.

'I'm sorry, Arya,' he said. 'I know that the Ramayana stories created a special bond between your mother and you. Perhaps it would do you good if you simply store them away in your memory like a buried treasure.'

I tried. I held on to them for as long as they remained alive in my mind. But every day brought new challenges and new battles in the schoolyard. The stories grew fainter until they became a distant reminder of happier days. Gone were the heroic acts of Rama and his army of vanaras. Perhaps they'd never existed.

~

A month after I'd stopped visiting Ma, Pa made an announcement.

'Arya, we need to talk,' he said.

I was doing my homework. I looked up at him. I could tell by the tone of Pa's voice that whatever he had to say wasn't going to be fun.

'I've been thinking,' he said slowly. 'This is not going to come easy but perhaps it is time we let her go.'

WHAT! These last few weeks I'd done everything I could to distance myself from the reality of Ma and her accident. Still, his words pierced through my heart with an inexplicable pain. It felt as though a thousand arrows had instantaneously struck me.

'You can't possibly be saying what I think you are saying!' I said.

'It's time to pull the plug, Arya.'

'No!' I said firmly. I pulled back my chair drawing away from Pa. 'That's moronic. You can't. WE can't!'

'I know it's not what you want to hear, Arya,' Pa said. 'Believe me, it's not what I'd ever wanted to say.'

'Ma is not just a mother,' I said. 'She's a rock. Without her, nothing is worth anything.'

'Arya, I ...'

But I didn't want to hear it. I threw down my pencil and stormed out of the kitchen to Ma's study room. All around me were shelves that housed her vast collection of books. Seized by some strange depravity, I began pulling out them at random and proceeded to leaf through them.

I couldn't even tell what I was looking for. Some inner voice urged me to search because I knew my quest would help me find an answer. It was Ma's eternal mantra. But, what the heck was I to search for? Satyajit Ray's poetry? The works of Swami Vivekananda? Ancient hymns of the Rig Veda?

Almost like a divine intervention, a ray of sunshine crept in through the skylight and cast its glow on one particular book, encircling it with a halo of liquid gold. It was a frayed leather-bound book with gilded writing on the cover—*The Ramayana*. Ma's copy, the one she read from every night. An out-of-print edition, musty, with delicate pages that had yellowed over time. Written in Sanskrit by Valmiki, one of the great sages of ancient India, the Ramayana told the story of Prince Rama of Ayodhya in 24,000 verses.

The verses written in Sanskrit brought back a familiar rush of warmth. As I thumbed through the pages, I could strangely feel Ma's presence in the room. I heard her laugh, I envisioned her smiling face, and took a whiff of her perfume from the musty pages of the book.

I ran my finger down the verses. Even though I didn't fully understand, I knew I was looking at the source of everything—the stories of my people, and the tribe from which we had originated. I was also searching for the endpoint.

'Ma, you can't leave me!' I said out loud. 'I can read the words, but I need you to help me understand them better. Otherwise what good is this Ramayana?'

Then again, from who knows what place, I heard her voice.

'The Ramayana takes you on a unique journey,' she said. '*Margadarshan*, a healing journey that shows you the road further. The source leads you along this road to the endpoint. But once you arrive there, you will find yourself back at the beginning, ready to start your journey again. And so, continue.'

That was exactly it! I flipped through to the end of the first chapter, 'As long as man lives upon Earth, the story of Rama shall be told.' The words almost jumped off the page. If the Ramayana did provide a healing journey then perhaps there was hope after all; maybe I could heal her with its stories. Why the heck had I stayed away from her all this time?

~

I raced back to the nursing home that afternoon to explain to Ma what I had found.

'It was wrong of me not to visit you for so long,' I said gazing down at her lifeless, ash-stricken face. 'I'm sorry. But look, I came across your copy of the Ramayana! I can read it to you now, just as you did to me.'

I searched for a flicker of response but all that moved was the heart-rate monitor, proving that despite her stillness, she was alive.

That's when it occurred to me that this was a futile exercise! To think I could fix her by reading her verses was a useless and purely rubbish idea! I picked up her alarm clock and threw it against the wall in a rage.

A nurse came running to see what the commotion was all about.

'What did you do that for?' she said. She shook her head at the pieces of metal and plastic that lay strewn all over the floor.

'It's just a waste of time,' I screamed in exasperation. 'Yesterday, I wondered how we would survive without her, but the truth is that we already are surviving!'

'She can still hear you, you know,' the nurse responded quietly.

'Oh, to hell with it!' I shouted. I was done with the stupid nursing home.

~

At home I slammed the front door behind me and disappeared up the stairs. Pa followed me.

'Arya, how about some dinner?' he asked standing outside my room.

'I don't want your lousy cooking!' I said, without thinking how my unkind words could hurt him. I didn't care about anything anymore.

~

I couldn't sleep that night. I lay in my bed listening to the waves of the Pacific Ocean beat against the northern shores of my home. I thought about the vanaras and wished that like them, I too, could become extinct. The wind howled over the bay. The redwood trees loomed menacingly outside my window. Misery cackled mercilessly, beckoning me with crooked fingers.

Suddenly, my bed began to quiver. Now if you live in San Francisco, earthquakes just naturally become part of your life. I was used to them so I lay still, waiting for it to pass. But the quiver turned to a shake and then to a shudder. Within moments, I heard a massive rumbling sound as my bed began to tremble beneath.

Oh gosh! Scenes of disaster flashed through my head. It was a hundred years since the city had been consumed by fire, caused by perhaps, the greatest earthquake of the last century. There was always talk that the Bay area was due for another massive quake, probably a deadlier one. Could this be it?

The entire room was shaking violently. Then, the floor underneath me heaved and tipped, stretching and cracking as if at any moment its wooden boards would come apart. Right then I remembered that our entire neighbourhood was situated on a major geographical fault line. It was something I'd known for years but had never really made sense of until that moment.

The room tilted, thrusting all the furniture to one side. Before I could think, I was flung into a corner. The floorboards, which now sagged dangerously, came apart at their seams to form a large crack right down the middle. My room was suddenly an image of chaos. The bookcase toppled over, scattering the books everywhere. They slid along the tilted floor and within moments, most of them had slipped through the fault. Then my desk, my rocking chair, my skateboard, tennis racket, chest of drawers, clothes, everything disappeared down the deep chasm in the centre of my room.

Then, the worst happened! I began to slide towards the fault. I reached out to grab something—anything—but there was nothing to anchor me. Only one book had somehow made its way to me. I grabbed it and clutched it to my chest, screaming for help. But no sound emerged—my voice was trapped inside my chest. It didn't matter, it was too late. An unfamiliar, gravitational force sucked me through the fault into an alarming black void. With a deep breath, I took one last look at my room and what used to be my world.

Through the Abyss

A strong magnetic force pulled me into a black, unfamiliar abyss. I wanted to yell but when I tried, the sound stalled inside my body.

Then came a resistance. It transformed the magnetic pull to something different—a liquid breeze. I was floating towards a rainbow-coloured light in the distance.

Where the heck was I? In the depths of the San Francisco Bay? It couldn't be; the Pacific Ocean was freezing, nothing compared to this warm, reassuring, almost tropical sensation!

The rainbow light swirled into a kaleidoscope of brilliantly-coloured patterns before evening out into a path that beckoned me to swim towards its crimson, orange and royal blue extravaganza. As I drew close, the colours swirled around, and then morphed into vivid yet familiar images—the mural on the school yard wall and the mural outside Rainbow grocery store.

Then, the patterns darkened into gliding silhouettes of banyan trees with thick, long roots that grew down from their branches. They looked like old men with beards of wisdom. And flying through them were monkeys!

The scene changed again, this time to a high-definition movie showing giant cliffs with towering precipices and majestic waterfalls streaming beyond the rainbows, far away. They were surrounded by trees filled with prickly fruits. I could taste their sweet nectar just by sniffing their fragrance.

Suddenly, I came upon a grassy hillock in the thick of a forestland, abundant with trees and wild grass, and magnificent snowcapped mountains in the distance. I'd landed in a painting—into the graffiti art on the walls of Rainbow grocery store.

A beam of sunlight shone down on the scene like a blessing from God. Had I died and gone to heaven? I must be dreaming! I closed my eyes to check but when I reopened them, nothing had changed.

Only then, I became conscious of a heavy-weight object in my hands—Ma's old copy of the Ramayana. The distinct aroma of her Ayurvedic oils trapped in its yellowed pages seemed stronger than it ever did back home.

Something rustled towards me. I don't remember ever having laid eyes on a creature so odd!

The Forest Hermit

Making a beeline for me through the wild grass was a skinny yet muscular man, dressed in nothing but a white loincloth and a pair of wooden slippers. His well-oiled mane of snowy-white hair contrasted with the rosy pink of his cheeks. It was tied back into a topknot with a single loose strand hanging down the back of his neck. His face was wrinkled with lines of wisdom, but even so, there was something about him that was sprightly and childlike—maybe his sparkly eyes that twinkled gingerly above his high cheekbones. An unkempt beard hung down from the tip of his chin on to his skinny, naked chest. In his right hand, he swung a long staff made of dark wood. His rapid gait suggested he was on an important mission.

'At last!' he said. 'Delays are unassailable, but have you brought it with you?'

Huh? What was the "it" he was referring to? And who exactly was he talking to?

I stared curiously at the odd-looking man whose defined upper body muscles were garlanded by a string of rudraksha beads, the same kind that my mother kept on her prayer table. Could he actually be talking to me?

As if to read my mind, the man came to a halt at the edge of the hillock.

'Well, do you see anybody else?' he asked.

What? I jerked my head back in shock.

How on earth had he known what I was thinking?

'Indeed the creatures of the forest are at hand, but at this moment, they halt at the seams of your peripheral vision.'

I scratched the cover of the book in my hands. What on earth did this strange guy mean?

'Hermit,' he said, setting down his staff. 'Hermit is more respectful nomenclature, don't you think, than *strange guy*.'

He had done it again. He'd read my thoughts as though they were being projected on a screen before his eyes.

'To answer your question, I've had many years of solitary practice in reading the minds of this great planet's creatures.'

The man *did* look exactly like a hermit, right out of a storybook but there was something special about him, something oddly familiar. And something quite—I had trouble putting my finger on it—regal. I looked closely into his eyes. They were grey at first, but, then as they drew me in, they changed to a blue-green colour, like tide pools along the Pacific Coast.

'Silence may be golden but you haven't learned that yet,' the hermit said. His eyes twinkled with familiar warmth.

I finally mustered up the gumption to say something. 'You are talking to *me*?'

'Could there be another?' he replied with a smile.

Okay, this was really weird.

'Another who?' I demanded.

'Another Arya.'

Whoa! How the heck did he know my name?

The old man chuckled. 'Lifetimes of experience have trained the hermit of the Wild Woods to recognise an Arya.'

He then twirled his staff slowly as a king might wield an orb, unleashing a faint, blue swirl of something into the atmosphere.

'Besides, you are the only one in existence right now.'

He sighed, and waved his staff around me examining me from head to toe, 'You'll do just fine.'

My head began to spin as I tried to process the hermit's words. What was with the freakish events of the past hour? The earthquake in my room, the strange forestland, this vaguely familiar hermit who acted like he was expecting my arrival—it didn't make any sense. I was cloaked by a momentary lapse of security.

'Where am I?' I asked, reducing my voice to a near whisper.

'Questions, questions,' the hermit repeated incredulously. 'In the Wild Woods, of course!'

He wielded his staff once again to release a faint blue glow that swished around him like raw energy. What *was* that?

And what were the Wild Woods? Why did they sound so familiar?

'A visual to jog your memory?' he asked. Without waiting for an answer, he waved his staff as if to paint on an invisible easel in the air between us. Out of nowhere, he drew a picture of Ma's Ramayana.

'A book in hand is worth its weight in gold, especially if it is the last one left!' he said.

Ma's Ramayana had slid from my grasp and now lay hidden between two blades of tall grass. Luckily, the gilded writing on the cover gleamed in the sunlight revealing the book's resting place.

Then something clicked in my head.

'The Wild Woods! That's the term Ma used to refer to the dreaded jungles where Rama fought the rakshasas, who plagued the people of the forest.'

'A description not entirely incorrect,' the hermit said.

'But it can't be,' I said. I tilted my head towards the book. 'The Wild Woods are from the Ramayana.'

'Or perhaps, the Ramayana is from them.' With another flash of his staff, he zapped the suspended image of the book, and then made it disappear.

I picked up Ma's copy of the Ramayana and dusted a blade of grass off its cover. My mind stirred as I recalled Ma's stories about the Wild Woods. No wonder the forestland had looked familiar. Ma—I missed her. I felt a pang of sadness inside my chest.

'Your description of the Wild Woods does not capture the entire truth,' the hermit said, pointing his staff toward a grove of trees in the distance.

Again, a stream of blue energy emanated from its end, this time conjuring up a powerful wind that wound its way through the treetops, separating the branches to reveal a city skyline that I knew so well.

'San Francisco!' I said excitedly. 'Home!'

'The Wild Woods are more than Rama's jungle battleground,' the hermit explained. 'They are where you go after you have crossed the depths of your mind. They are the land on the other side, where your knowledge comes alive and learning becomes real.'

But I was too distracted by the sight of home to pay attention. My mind's eye saw a fleeting image of Ma sitting in her prayer room meditating upon the Ramayana. But then the image shifted to another gruesome picture of her lying pale and near-lifeless in her hospital bed. Uggh!

The hermit drew his staff away from the grove, reuniting the branches to reveal nothing but a dense growth of trees in what looked like a placid forest.

'Wait!' I said, overtaken by a sudden sense of urgency. 'What are you doing? I need to go back.'

But the old man looked wistfully into the distance without responding.

'Did you hear me?' I squealed. 'I need to wake my mother up from her coma.'

With the agility of a cheetah, the hermit leapt high into the air and landed back into a deep lunge, his arms stretched out to the sky and his hands clasped together in prayer. I recognised the warrior stance from Ma's endless yoga sessions.

'I need to save her first,' I said. I pulled my arms around my back to hide my shaking hands.

'You need to save yourself,' the hermit replied. 'And understand the ways of an Arya.'

'What do you mean?' I asked, opening my eyes wide.

The hermit chuckled, his eyes twinkling even more as he emerged from his warrior pose.

'There was a reason after all, that Rama and his brothers were brought here. They were taught the methods of archery and the use of asthra.'

'Asthra? As in weapons powered by divine mantras?'

The hermit nodded. 'A warrior needs to be trained in the environment that puts his weapons to use against the ferocity of dangerous surroundings. The palace at Ayodhya, Rama's home, would hardly be a suitable place for them to master these skills.'

He was referring to the story of how Rama and his brothers left their palace for the forest to apprentice with the great warrior sage Rishi Vishvamitra who trained them to fight against the forest demons. I opened the Ramayana in my hands to these early chapters and recognised the characters, the setting, and the references to mantra and archery.

There was one big difference though. The place that Ma referred to as the Wild Woods was somewhere in India, but I had arrived through a fault in the earth on which San Francisco stood.

The hermit chuckled again.

'Boy, you might come from anywhere but remember, things happen the way they need to happen.'

Boy. I recognised the expression but couldn't think from where.

'You aren't making any sense. *What* exactly needs to *happen?*'

'Sometimes, you have to fall through the fault line in your world,' the hermit replied.

'Me?'

'You. Or Rama, for that matter.'

Huh? I looked at him suspiciously. I'd been through plenty of years listening to Rama's stories. Never had there been any mention of him falling through a fault line.

The hermit's tide pool eyes widened before changing colour from bright blue to a wizened grey.

'The very purpose of Rama's existence requires him to fall through faults continuously.'

Why did he insist on this confusing talk?

'Look, all I need is to get back home,' I said impatiently. 'Can you help?'

'Boy,' the hermit said. 'Home is always just around the corner.'

'My home is in San Francisco!' I said, waving my book indignantly. 'With Pa and my Ma, who I have to save.'

'Then, you must complete your journey.'

'Exactly! Can you show me the way?'

'It's in your hands.'

What? All that was in my hands was Ma's Ramayana.

'Precisely. But as I have said before, it's the *last one left*,' continued the hermit. 'Which means that if it does fall into other hands, the wrong ones, then neither you nor anyone else can ever learn the rightful ways of an Arya. Yet, no journey can be completed without passing through the Dark Side.'

Again, I grappled with the meaning of his words. As I did, the hermit's appearance began to change. His body slowly morphed into a fuzzy blue image that began to fade into the background. Thinking something must be wrong with my eyes, I rubbed them, but when I looked again I saw it was true. The hermit was now a faint blue shadow silhouetted against the dark green trees.

'Wait,' I said, focusing deep into the hermit's blue-green eyes. 'Have we met before?'

By then the hermit's silhouette had disappeared too. Only his voice rang out through the trees.

'That, my boy, is for me to know and for you to find out.'

'What do you mean?'

But, there was no answer. I stood alone in the Wild Woods.

~

The truth of the situation wrapped itself around me like a giant web binding me to the dense forest. Here I was, alone in a strange land with no idea how to return home.

'What do I do now?' I said out loud to a cluster of wild flowers. As if in response, they blew a gust of wind my way.

Of course! I recalled Ma's calming words. I needed to take ten breaths, deep enough to allay my insecurities and fears.

As I inhaled deep into my belly, I noticed the intensity of the kaleidoscopic life in the forest. Every conceivable colour intermingled before me and seemed at first like a wild, unruly array, but as I looked closer, I was amazed to see a brilliant pattern of organisation. Red, yellow and deep purple butterflies flitted about the pink florescence while yellow and black bees buzzed about the lavender-coloured stalks. Then, a beautiful black-and-red bird hovered over the bright yellow sunflowers that danced away in a breeze.

I smiled. 'There was a scene from the epic when Rama had paused in the thick of his martial arts practice to soak in the natural beauty of his surroundings!' I said to the bird.

Seized by a magical spell, the pages of the book fluttered, inviting me to open them to the scene. It took a few moments, but with some concentrated effort I recalled the chapter—

Rama stood in the thick of the forest, his bow strung to his arrow. He closed his eyes to inhale the healing essence of the medicinal plants. Then, he opened them to imbibe the hue of healing.

My eyes came to rest on a long green shoot with millions of tiny orange and white buds cylindrically arranged. The shoot closely resembled a broom. Something ticked inside my head. The hermit's tide pool eyes—Niklas had exactly the same!

I recognised his white hair sparkling in the afternoon sunlight as he cleaned the yard. Those changing tide pool eyes were unmistakably his. The hermit *was* the janitor. I was certain.

A voice rang out from somewhere in the forest.

'Speculation is the key to comprehension.'

I looked around, but couldn't see him anywhere. I figured I could cover all bases by projecting my voice into the centre of the forest ahead. 'Niklas, is that you?'

No response. I tried again.

'Hermit, did you take a janitorial job at my school?'

'Our jobs are not to take or leave. Neither yours nor mine,' the voice answered. 'They are given to us for a specific purpose.'

I looked up at the sky, squinting as the sun's rays caught the corner of my eyes.

'I don't have a job.'

Although, he was nowhere to be seen, the hermit replied in a definite tone.

'We all have jobs. Several, that change with time.'

'Time?'

'The thing that differs from one moment to the next. Theory of Relativity, boy.'

The hermit's silhouette began to take shape in the space before me. His words were still awfully confusing.

'You said I needed to go through the Dark Side to complete my journey. But what does that even mean?'

'As I said before, it's in your hands,' the hermit replied.

I became distinctly aware of the book weighing down in my palms, and recalled Ma's words during so many bedtime stories—

'It is the rakshasa in you that sets off your destructive nature sucking you into the Dark Side. You must try to quell your rakshasa mind.'

'It doesn't make sense,' I shouted into the trees. 'You can't have a rakshasa mind if you're a human.'

The hermit's silhouette moved to a tree branch directly in my line of vision. Gradually he came into focus, balanced upon one leg with his arms stretched up and into the air, what Ma referred to as a perfect tree pose. How could he possibly keep his balance without opening his eyes?

'Practice makes perfect,' the hermit answered. 'Tell me though, how does a boy with a rakshasa mind speak with such conviction about the nature of rakshasa mind?'

A thorn of irritability pricked my insides. How dare he insinuate that I had the mind of a rakshasa!

I opened my mouth to speak, but couldn't really find the words to describe what I wanted to say.

The hermit sensed my problem and decided to help.

'Let's look at the definition of a rakshasa.'

Like a high-speed train, I blurted out something from memory.

'A rakshasa is an awful demon who eats humans and animals and strikes terror among them. It's huge, twice as tall as an average man, with multi-coloured blood, sharp talons and mandibles that look like those of a giant insect.'

As I rattled on, the hermit used his staff to draw an image of the demon I described on a canvas of thin air.

'Some look like giant cobras,' I continued, 'with human heads and torsos, but forked tongues and serpentine lower bodies and tails. Others resemble enormous reptiles, with swollen lumps covering their ugly and unpleasant skin. There are demons who have hooves and some of them have horns too. And some can even change at will.'

Where the heck had I pulled this description from?

The hermit had drawn the image of a rakshasa with a serpentine body, swollen lumps and horns. He tapped his staff on to the demon horns, instantly replacing its ugly head with a familiar face that was beautiful to look at on first glance.

My eyes widened as I gasped and drew the connection to Athena. Whoa!

I said, 'No matter what they look like, their purpose is the same: to strike terror among humans and animals, and to do what they can to ruin our lives.'

'A parrot memory no doubt,' the hermit said. 'A verbatim description of rakshasas from the epic.'

I couldn't say anything. I was reeling from the realisation that I'd just recited by heart, the ultimate description of the very thing that I had pined to be a part of all along—a member of The Boys.

'In fact, so etched are these verses in your psyche, they have the potential to influence your every action. A perfect platform for your job ahead.'

A fireball of anger rushed up my insides. I was strangely invigorated as I became aware of a strong urge to destroy rakshasas.

'Ah, but a desire to destroy is the very tendency of the rakshasa mind!' the hermit said.

'Rakshasas are demons. How can an urge to destroy demons be considered demonic?' I pouted.

The forest hermit stroked his beard and pulled himself out of his tree pose. Then with a wave of his staff, he cleared the image of the rakshasa from the space in front of us, replacing it with wisps of blue energy that quickly dissipated into the air.

'Reaction is a sorry excuse for action,' he said. 'A real Arya would know this when he has completed his journey.'

'I *am* real!' I shouted. 'And I really need to be done with this journey! I have a task to accomplish at home.'

The hermit didn't react. With another stroke of his beard, he jumped down from the tree branch.

'Your first task boy,' he said, 'for you have more than one, is to keep this last copy of the book in your hands far away from those who want it. You owe it to your fellow beings.'

Another rustling sound drew my attention. Through the distant trees emerged a shadow of two humans. They were small, the size of boys. As the shadows contorted, I deciphered the shape of two long tails. Perhaps, they weren't humans after all. Tree monkeys? No, they couldn't be. Tree monkeys were usually smaller. Maybe they were gorillas, or apes, but then they had tails.

I wanted to investigate the shadows. Perhaps, their owners could show me the way out, but they vanished as quickly as they had appeared.

'Wait, the Ramayana? Who wants it?' I asked.

But the hermit didn't answer. He sprang forward like an arrow from a bow. 'Ah, I must be gone. I will see you again.'

When he turned to wave goodbye, his features had changed—his wrinkles had melted into the focused visage of a young warrior-in-training and his large blue-green tide pool eyes beckoned me.

I blinked, thinking I must be daydreaming.

'Dream on,' the hermit laughed. 'Dreams provide a glimpse of your inner self.' Then he disappeared out of sight behind the trees.

Chimpu and Pandu

The book in my hands seemed heavier than ever, weighing upon me the reality that perhaps in all these years it had been my safe haven. My arrival in this land of its stories couldn't possibly be a twist of fate. The Ramayana was filled with Rama's various exploits, rescuing the Aryas from the hands of evil. Surely, I too could learn how to use it to rescue Ma from the evil hands of illness. For gosh sake, I had landed in the story, all I needed to do was to live it.

I walked through the forest for what seemed like several minutes or probably an hour. Maybe more. The sun was setting when I arrived at a valley surrounded by wild apple trees unevenly strewn on gentle slopes. Yellowed fallen leaves formed a plushy carpet under my feet. Dewdrops glistened from the grass that peeped from between the dried leaves on the ground.

The air around me was dense with the fragrance of apple blossoms. The white petals reminded me of home. Each spring, Ma would prepare her famous digestive drink from the essence of apple blossoms. And in the fall, I'd gather the fruit so she could prepare apple halwa, her unique Ayurvedic take on the all-American apple pie. She served it each year at Thanksgiving. Life was certainly not as bad as I had thought it had been.

I stopped to examine an unusual looking plant with a large tube-like opening, sitting atop a hillock. It swayed gently towards the insects that flew by, surprisingly resembling a Hawaiian hula dancer! A large fly hovered near the tube searching for a place to rest. Slowly, the tube moved ever so slightly towards the insect. At first, I thought I was imagining it, but then, the plant stretched its tube, opening it like a mouth, enticing the insect to enter. Once the fly did that, the tube snapped its lips around the insect. A few moments later when the plant opened its mouth again, the insect was gone, swallowed deep into the plant's thick and thorny stem. A venus flytrap! It began to sway once again, gently in the breeze, perfectly innocent.

A rustling sound from the trees caught my attention. Within moments, it was amplified by a chittering noise. Then, right before my eyes, two furry, monkey-like creatures with long scraggy tails and bright red bottoms scampered down onto the grass. One of them had tan fur covering his body and the other had almost white fur. Monkeys? I'd seen plenty—langurs, chimpanzees, orangutans, thanks to my glorious summer job taking care of the primates at the San Francisco Zoo. But, I'd never seen or read about a species like this. These monkeys looked less like monkeys and more like little boys with tails. I watched as they wagged their tails in delight.

The tan creature spoke with a big smile on his face, 'I'm Chimpu.'

Then, he pointed to his pale companion. 'This is my friend, Pandu. We've been waiting for you.'

Holy camoly! Since when could monkeys talk? But wait, they weren't really monkeys. Were they the shadows I'd seen earlier? Before I could entertain the thought any further, the voice of the hermit resounded through the leaves, 'You owe it to your fellow beings.'

All this time, I'd been wondering what he meant by *fellow beings*, but right then, it made sense. The pages of the Ramayana fluttered magically once again in my hands, as if to beckon me to search for clarification. I flipped through its pages when a hazy thought struck me. My eyes came to rest at the scene in which Rama and his brother, Lakshmana, first met the vanaras.

I heard Ma's voice in my head, '*Vanara is a Sanskrit word, meaning a human who has the fur and tail of a monkey. They are not like ordinary monkeys. They are brave and inquisitive humanoids that have descended from the simian races.*'

Vanaras had formed an army of thousands under the leadership of Hanumana to help Rama win his battle against Ravana. Vanaras, a foot shorter than the average human being, with fur covering their bodies, stood right here in front of me, talking to me as though I was one of them. My *fellow beings*.

The hermit spoke again.

'Inquisitive, loyal, and bluntly honest, your fellow beings mirror your own values. Look into the book and you shall see.' Funny, the vanaras chittered endlessly, they didn't seem to hear any of his words.

'When we saw your delight at the temperamental ways of the plants in the Wild Woods, we knew it must be you,' Pandu explained.

I squinted at them through the rays of the sun setting behind. The Ramayana described vanaras as amusing and mildly irritating, though unbelievably courageous in their efforts to help Rama. Could they possibly also help me?

'Guru*ji* said you'd be coming, Arya,' Chimpu added.

Guru*ji*? I recognised the respectful title. Chimpu must be talking about the hermit, I thought. At the mention of his name, both vanaras erected their tails upright in respect. And Arya—were they talking about me? Or did they use the word 'Arya' to refer to my clansmen in the story of the Ramayana?

'Do you mean the disappearing hermit?' I asked.

'Guru*ji* appears and then disappears,' Pandu replied. 'Sometimes you see all of him, sometimes only a part of him and at other times, all you hear is his voice.'

'He behaves more like a sorcerer than a sage,' I said.

'He's actually a bit of both,' Chimpu said. 'Sages like him have been infused with Brahman Shakti for thousands of years.'

'Brahman Shakti?' I asked. 'What's that?'

The two vanaras looked at each other incredulously.

'After so long, an Arya has finally arrived in the Wild Woods, but you do not know the meaning of Brahman Shakti?' Chimpu asked. I never forgot the look on his face at that moment.

My muscles tensed in embarrassment, but then I relaxed as I heard Ma's voice in my head again.

'Brahman Shakti is the essence of creation, responsible for the ebb and flow of all life on earth. Each of us is infused with its latent power but only the chosen few are able to harness it.'

I wanted to ask Chimpu and Pandu more about Brahman Shakti but they'd already lost interest in the conversation. They now pranced around me, examining me from head to toe.

'How does an Arya keep warm without fur?' Pandu asked. He snatched the Ramayana from my hands, flipped through the first few pages and then held it up excitedly.

'Look,' he said to Chimpu. 'The Arya has brought the book with him!' Both vanaras began to chitter, dismayed.

'What's wrong?' I asked.

'It would have been safer had you left it at home,' Chimpu said, scratching his head.

'Why?'

'It's what *they* want!' Pandu said looking nervous.

'Who?' My interest was piqued.

But, the vanaras seemed edgy and quickly changed the subject.

'We've been stalking you since you arrived this morning,' Chimpu said.

'Stalking me?' I tensed up, suddenly on guard.

'Don't be alarmed,' Chimpu said. 'We did it only out of curiosity and with good intention. When we saw Guru*ji* talking to you, we knew it was safe.

I slowly processed all I knew thus far. Guru*ji* was a sage who had foretold my arrival in the Wild Woods; the vanaras had closely followed my whereabouts. Was all this really happening?

I cleared my throat to speak, 'Why would the Ramayana be safer at home?'

The vanaras threw skittish glances at each other.

'If *they* know you have it, then they'll make life even more difficult.'

Okay, this was getting annoying. I had no clue what they were going on about.

'Who are *they* and why are *they* so interested in the book?' I demanded, impatiently.

Chimpu darted up and grabbed my hand and said, 'Baalchorni, the jungle rakshasi, scares us to bits. She's the most evil demon in this part of the forest. She's been sent here to look for the book, but all she does is torture our children and destroy our homes. We used to live in Kishkindha, you know, in the southern part of the forestlands, but thanks to Baalchorni, we have now become nomads. We have to wander to protect our little ones from her.'

Pandu held my other hand. 'Even now, we have been told that the world just passes us off as imaginary creatures. Our numbers have dwindled and we are in danger of going extinct.'

He looked earnestly into my eyes, 'We need your help.'

I couldn't believe what I'd just heard. All this time I had assumed that the vanaras could help *me*, but now the tables had turned and they were asking for *my* help! But for what?

'If we cease to exist, then who shall remain to bear Hanumana's flag?' Chimpu asked. 'All monkeys love and honour our great leader, but only the vanara race is capable of forming his army.' Hanumana's flag! I looked intently into the eyes of both vanaras.

'Where is Hanumana? Is he also here in the Wild Woods?' I asked.

'Hanumana has taken a hiatus,' Chimpu answered. 'He is spending time in the abode of his spiritual father, Vayu, the Lord of Wind.'

A shiver of distress crept up my spine. 'Does that mean he's dead?'

Contrary to my expectations, the two vanaras burst into a fit of laughter.

'Hanumana dead? No, goodness! That is not even possible. He is gifted with the power to wander the forestlands for as long as they exist.'

Despite the vanaras' visible happiness, I had to say, I was unnerved by their words. Hanumana might live as long as the forestlands exist but this didn't mean the forests would last forever. Back home on the western shores of America, the ancient redwood trees once sprawled across the continent, but now they only stretched from Oregon to Big Sur. Some of them were a 1, 000-years-old, yet they had been felled relentlessly to provide wood for the decks of fancy houses. How long *could* forestlands actually exist and what did that mean for Hanumana and the vanaras?

Chimpu continued, 'It's just that he has entrusted his earthly work to us, at least for some time, while he rejuvenates himself under the blessing of his father's house.'

'His earthly work?'

The two vanaras nodded at each other, 'Come,' Pandu said, 'We'll show you.'

They scampered through the trees at a pace that forced me to run in order to keep up.

We trampled over the knee-high grasses and through the shrubs, sending fruits and berries flying in all directions. Even wild elephants would have made a neater job of traversing the jungle pathways.

Moments later, we arrived at what looked like a natural jungle-gym. Scores of banyan trees with big suspended roots stood throughout this part of the forest. Chimpu and Pandu swung from tree to tree using the roots like swings in a gymnasium.

Huddled in the mesh of branches were vanaras of every possible shape and size—old vanaras with wrinkled faces, young and energetic vanaras and mothers, holding furry babies peeping out from behind the leaves. All with different shades of fur ranging from white to dark tan, all had distinct red faces and bottoms like Chimpu and Pandu.

As soon as they became aware of our arrival, they began to clap, screech and chitter. How was I supposed to respond to something like this? I'd never seen anything like it before.

When things calmed down, my eye caught a triangular saffron-coloured flag fluttering high at the top of the tallest tree in the centre of the jungle-gym. The wonder must have been apparent in my expression.

'Hanumana's flag,' Pandu explained, 'stands for stability, equilibrium and mind control.'

'And, a sure sign of the victory of good over evil,' Chimpu chimed in.

The Appeal of the Sourcebook

It was time to eat and I was starving.

'What do you folks do for grub around here?' I asked Chimpu.

'Nuts, fruits and plenty of herbs,' he replied. 'Community meals are an important aspect of vanara life. We are happy as long as Baalchorni doesn't grace us with her presence.'

I scratched my head trying to rationalise this. Fruits and nuts did not seem ripe for a demon diet. 'I thought rakshasis were carnivorous.'

'They are,' Chimpu replied, scratching his tummy out of hunger.

'So what's her fascination with boring things like nuts and fruits?'

A group of vanaras gathered around me, shooting uneasy glances at each other. Okay, okay, I had put my foot in my mouth. I rephrased my words.

'No offence, I am sure it tastes great. It's just that, I didn't think rakshasis could be vegetarians.'

'They're not,' an old vanara said slowly. He was Buddha, the leader of the tribe. By his name, I knew that wisdom was on his side.

'So, why are you worried about Baalchorni then?'

'Because it's us that she's after—'

'Our little ones,' Buddha replied.

Wait, I thought she'd been sent to look for the book! Before I could ask more questions, a hooting noise rang out in the jungle-gym. It was the dinner call. Hundreds of vanaras leapt down from the branches of a massive tree in the centre of the jungle-gym for a grand meal. I casually put my book down on a thick branch, which displeased Buddha.

'It's too valuable,' he said. 'We can't risk it falling into the forest below. Who knows where it might land or who might find it?'

Chimpu found a niche in a tree trunk that served as a placeholder.

'It'll be safe as a secret here,' he said.

Dinner consisted of nuts and fruits, both of which turned out to be not so boring after all, and a drink extracted from honeycombs. The fresh aroma of the warm, golden liquid took me back to happy memories of Ma's cooking.

'What's this?' I asked, swirling the honey drink around on my tongue.

'It's the essence of bee pollen,' Pandu replied. 'The perfect elixir to soothe your nerves.'

'Perfect' perhaps for hyper vanaras—I wasn't so sure about drinking bee pollen, but decided to give it a go. As I sipped the drink, a warm energy spread through my body. It was like a magic potion that opened the doors of my mind.

'Isn't it the best?' Chimpu asked, his face lit with a contented smile. I nodded, unable to speak as the warm, dense drink spread its sweetness down to my gut. One by one, the vanaras introduced themselves drawing me into the details of their existence. It was hard to recall them all, I couldn't remember their names or even understand their chittering, but in those few hours, we just took to each other, like we'd discovered old ties from a previous existence.

'You've taken to the honey drink,' Buddha said, rubbing his tummy and letting out a loud burp. 'You *do* know that only those with a unique genetic code from the Old World Tribes can digest it.'

I pondered over Buddha's words as he took another sip. Of course, it made perfect sense. Ma had always insisted that humans and vanaras came from a common ancestor of simpler times named by zoology books as the Old World Monkey.

After the meal, the warm energy began to fade, but I was pleasantly sated. It was time to ask the vanaras for help.

'How do I find my way home?' I asked. 'I need to go back to my Ma. She is in a coma, and it was all my fault.'

The vanaras looked at each other, confused and dismayed.

'Look, I feel awful about the whole thing,' I continued. 'And, when I had a chance to try and heal her with the stories from the Ramayana, I didn't. I was just angry about everything.'

The relatively calm jungle-gym was instantly transformed into a circus of hyperactivity as the vanaras resumed their high-pitched chittering and began to beat their tails against the branches nervously.

'What's your deal?' I asked, annoyed.

'You can't go. You've just arrived!' Chimpu exclaimed. His eyes appeared to be growing larger by the minute. It was obviously the effect of the honey wine.

'Look, I've had fun hanging out with you, but my Ma is very sick,' I insisted. 'They are planning to pull the plug in just a few days from now. I need to get back and do my best to cure her.'

The vanaras' chitter rose to a loud din. Uh oh, now what?

'Hush!' Buddha said. 'Let's explain.' He sucked in a deep breath and then let out a long sigh.

The vanaras began to talk and little by little, and I began to understand their problem. Baalchorni had been after their blood for a long time. She would periodically show up to capture, kill and eat their young.

'She is a direct threat to our survival,' said Ranga, another vanara, nervously. 'But her Master is a direct threat to life itself.'

'Her Master?' I asked, curious to know who could possibly evoke such fear.

The vanaras looked at each other with alarm.

'Could an Arya with the sourcebook really be asking this question?' Chimpu asked.

I guess my dumbfounded expression didn't help.

'Why, the most evil of all the rakshasas!' Pandu answered.

I opened my eyes wide, 'Ravana?'

The vanaras nodded. None of them could bring themselves to say his name.

'Ravana, the ten-headed demon king of Lanka?' I enquired again. 'Are you sure?'

The vanaras nodded again, casting their eyes towards the jungle floor.

It was impossible! I grabbed my book from its resting place, relying less this time on the magic of its pages. As they fluttered before me, I knew exactly which chapter to turn to.

'Ravana is dead!' I said. 'It's written right here. Rama killed him by shooting an arrow to his navel.'

Raja, a vanara with a bright white streak running down the top of his head all the way to his mid-back, scampered down to me and took my hand.

'When Ravana is killed, he sinks to the depths of the netherworld. He stays there for a long, long time so that goodness is given a chance to replenish itself in society. But much as we all would love it, good times do not last forever.'

They certainly didn't. I knew this better than anyone else.

'It doesn't make any sense though,' I cried. 'Why wouldn't they last?'

'It's against the rules of the universe,' Buddha said, putting his arm around me. But I wasn't comforted.

'Still doesn't make any sense,' I repeated firmly.

A streak of blue lightning flashed through the jungle skies, sending a group of young vanaras scampering off in fright. The older, more mature ones however, remained calm. They were obviously accustomed to these sudden streaks of electricity.

'The universe makes sense only out of nonsense, and that boy, is one of the few things that make perfect sense,' a familiar voice echoed.

It was Guru*ji*. He came into view from the streak of lightning and stood in front of the vanaras.

'If good was always good, then there would be too much good, which would be no good at all, for it is the pull and push between bad and good that maintains the natural order of the universe.'

Once again, I had no idea what he was saying. Guru*ji* began to silently count the rudraksha beads in his hand.

But I wanted to make sense of what the vanaras had told me.

'Has Ravana come back to *life*?' I asked.

'Goodness will quell badness until such time as the forces of evil rise up from the netherworld again to enter the battle zone,' Guru*ji* answered.

I went over his words slowly in my head.

'So, Ravana *has* come back to life.'

'Or has life come back to the ways of Ravana?' Guru*ji* asked. His eyes sparkled in the evening moonlight.

'But why? What could he possibly want?' I knew it couldn't be Sita, Rama's wife. 'Does he want to extinguish the vanara tribe?' I asked.

'That and worse,' replied Pandu, 'He wants the book itself.'

'The book?' I asked, puzzled.

'The epic in your hands,' Guru*ji* explained wryly in between his counting.

I glanced at the yellowed pages of Ma's Ramayana, still on the verse in which Rama killed Ravana, and tried to fathom his words. Sure, this was the sourcebook that recorded the history of the Aryas, and of the triumph of Rama over Ravana—good over evil. But why did Ravana need it?

Guru*ji* stopped counting the beads and looked me straight in the eye.

'Because history is created only at its source.'

I looked back at him blankly. What on earth was he talking about? The vanaras began to chitter loudly again until Chimpu spoke above the din.

'Ravana wants to erase the history completely, to prove that good never existed. To show that he was always all powerful, and then use this falsehood to slowly gain his control over the lands.'

I gulped hard, signs of disbelief obviously spreading over my face. Chimpu shook his head sadly.

'Ravana has been waiting for the book ever since he re-emerged from the netherworld to strike terror once again. There are no more copies left in the Wild Woods, he has destroyed them all. You have the very last one, Arya.'

What? Was Ma's faded copy of the Ramayana really the last one left?

Guru*ji* spoke again. 'The book you hold is the proof that these vanaras and all good creatures of the Wild Woods need to be preserved—as evidence of the history that Ravana was erased.'

For the first time, I understood what Guru*ji* was trying to say. The warmth of the honey drink fuelled a fire somewhere inside my heart. Ravana had always been the enemy, but this time, it was different. There was no Rama, there was no Sita to save. I looked around at the hundreds of vanaras staring back at me. My gaze then fixed on Buddha, the old vanara leader.

'Arya, we need your help,' he said.

Arya. Ma's voice rang in my consciousness like temple bells signifying an evening prayer—

'Arya. Protector of the People. Remember that you were named for a reason.'

'Advice from our ancestors is the fountain of our success,' Guru*ji* added.

I pictured Ma lying strapped to a life-support machine. This last copy of the book was supposed to help me heal her, it couldn't get into Ravana's hands under any cost. But why was there no Rama? And where was Hanumana?

Guru*ji*'s gaze pierced the depths of my insides. 'Quell your internal inflammation and you will find Rama.'

'Control your mind and you will find Hanumana.'

He started fiddling with his beads once again. At first glance, he appeared to be counting numbers, but on looking closer, I saw that he was repeating a mantra with each bead.

I recounted Guru*ji*'s words from the moment we'd met. 'When you walk the earth for thousands of years,' he'd said. How could he possibly be that old?

Something dawned upon me– if Guru*ji* had truly walked the earth for thousands of years, and if this forest was truly the habitat of Rama's adventures, then there was only one person he could possibly be—Rishi Vishvamitra, one of the most venerated sages of ancient India.

As these thoughts raced through my head, a faint blue glow began emanating outwards from his body. Brahman Shakti. Chimpu and Pandu had spoken about it. The image of Guru*ji* faded into a grey silhouette. The next moment, he had completely vanished.

'Guru*ji*,' I said, jumping up. 'Who are you? How did you find me?'

A muffled voice reverberated from the distance, like the sound of an echo in a large cave.

'Who found who, boy? I think it was you who found me.'

I couldn't identify the direction of the voice. Once again, the great Guru*ji* was gone.

The Weapon of Fire

I set off through the trees in the hope of finding Guru*ji* again. A rush of energy spread through my body as I inhaled the forest air infused with the aroma of wild plants. It was even stronger than Ma's garden at home in San Francisco.

I heard a voice behind me.

'What is most admirable about a skilled storyteller is that he leaves wide scope for possibility, which is after all the very purpose of imagination.'

I turned to see the hermit balanced on a tree branch in a perfect dhanurasana, a yoga posture that mimicked the curve of a bow. His left leg swerved out behind him and was clutched by his left arm, while his upper body and right arm pointed straight ahead. He looked different from before, dressed in a saffron-coloured dhoti. His staff, no longer made of striped wood, resembled the golden wand of a sorcerer. But most importantly, his right arm was emblazoned with a tattoo that spelled Vishvamitra in Sanskrit. How could I have missed this earlier?

'So it's true,' I said studying the tattoo. 'It wasn't just my imagination.'

'Balance, boy,' Guru*ji* answered, perfectly still on the tree branch, 'is the recipe for focus.' Then, with meticulous precision, he released his yoga posture, bringing both feet to the branch. 'Only if you imagine something first, can you eventually realise it.'

He jumped to the ground with the grace of a feline creature, 'When you have done so, then you have mastered it.'

I stepped forward, excited.

'Rishi Vishvamitra, I thought you died ages ago!'

Guru*ji* was amused. 'You and thousands of others,' he laughed. 'Why does your generation rely on assumption when research is pin-pointedly preferable?' he asked.

But, I was too thrilled with my discovery to stop.

'But the Ramayana happened almost 7, 000 years ago. Where did it say that you'd still be alive?'

Guru*ji* tapped the tip of his staff, his grey eyes changed to an incandescent blue.

'What part of history records the details of my death?'

He was right. Although most of the ancient scriptures referred to the long lives of the ancient seers, very few of them actually recorded their deaths.

'What does that mean about the other seers of ancient times? Do they also walk the earth like you?'

Guru*ji* stepped onto a moss-covered rock and settled into a seated lotus position. He stared silently at me, his blue eyes glowing in the dark forest.

'Twelve immortals of Indic wisdom have traversed the planet since the days of Rama,' he said. 'Each awaits the opportunity to work with the next Arya.'

A shiver that had nothing to do with heat or cold crept up my spine.

'Hanumana has been waiting,' Guru*ji* continued.

I saw an image take shape in the dark core of Guru*ji*'s eyes. It was the image of the seasoned vanara general with a long tail waving in slow motion—Hanumana!

'Only an Arya can restore meaning to the history of these forests,' Guru*ji* said, his eyes turning a deep turquoise blue.

I was drawn into the Rishi's turquoise eyes with a magnetic attraction that took me away from the dark forest.

'The Aryas were noble people who lived to serve others around them. Rama was an Arya. He saved these forests and its people from the demons. Now after all these years here you are, an Arya who has descended from the warrior race. Your name stands true to your purpose.'

The mention of Rama and the 'warrior race' transported me once again to Ma's hospital bed. I gazed into her ashen face as I listened to Guru*ji*'s voice echoing in the background. She'd never talked about Pa's background much, but this I knew—Ma belonged to the lineage of Aryas.

'Will this be the Arya to save a history that is in danger of being erased?' Guru*ji* asked. His words echoed through my being.

An electrifying energy coursed through my body. Finally, I absorbed the reality of my mother's sickness and standing in the small, stark hospital room, it became clear to me that my arrival in the Wild Woods was not a coincidence. It was a journey to heal something larger even than her, a journey to help the vanaras and secure the history of my clansmen. I must complete the larger journey before going home to Ma.

'If the story of the Ramayana itself is destroyed, then how will you heal your mother?' Guru*ji* asked.

He was right. Its verses, after all, provided the medicine that might do the trick.

Guru*ji* transposed me back into the dark forest. Ma's hospital bed slowly faded like an old memory.

'*This* Arya will,' I said with new resolution. 'I am the Protector of the People.' I clutched my Ramayana tightly to my chest.

Guru*ji* smiled, 'Then, it is time for *this* Arya to be inducted into the Vedic martial arts,' he said.

He closed his eyes and moved his arms around as if in a trance. The faint blue glow of Brahman Shakti, the raw energy which had earlier wafted from his staff, now streamed from his finger tips. The glow intensified with each move and gradually concentrated into a bright ball of blue sparkle that he balanced on his right ring finger. Out of this ball, he slowly formed a shiny, black cast iron bow. It probably weighed a ton but Guru*ji* balanced it on the tips of his fingers, like a feather.

'A warrior must be iron clad,' he said, spinning the bow like a majorette. 'Strength reaches infinite levels when a warrior is in possession of the asthra.'

Asthra! The Weapon. All the references to asthra that I had ever heard about were from the Ramayana and they were all related to divine weapons.

The Ramayana described how Rama, endowed with the powerful weapons infused with Brahman Shakti, had managed to quell an entire battalion of rakshasas. The Brahmasthra was the all-powerful weapon of Lord Brahma, creator of the universe, and it was Rishi Vishvamitra who had taught Rama the art of warfare.

'The Brahmasthra is an advanced divine weapon, handed over to those who spend years in training under their guru,' he said. 'The days of the gurukul, the glorious tradition of gurus who retreated to forest schools with their *kul,* their family of students, have long since been abandoned.'

Indeed, Rama had spent many years apprenticing under his guru. As the Protector of his people, he had no choice but to become master, never once questioning his guru's authority.

'Are you asking me to apprentice for seven years?' I asked curiously.

'These days, the seven seers recognise the need to make adjustments,' Guru*ji* said, bringing the bow to a halt.

'Weaponry is essential for self-defence. The asthras are selected for suitability. A young boy with an inquiring mind and an internal fire, must fight fire with fire.'

Guru*ji* set down the bow on the grass. It sparkled like a band of solid gold kissed by sunlight. He began to chant a mantra, ending with the words, 'Agneyasthra.'

Agneyasthra—the ancient, divine Weapon of Fire. The words clung to me like tight fitting armour. Guru*ji* opened his eyes.

'Take heed though, a warrior who goes to battle with an intention to destroy cannot be the warrior of the Aryas.'

But my mind was focused on Agneyasthra. Fighting with fire. What a unique idea!

'Easy now,' Guru*ji* said. 'The Agneyasthra can be highly destructive if used with evil intent. You cannot be given the entire asthra, only a small portion, enough to equip you with what you need for your battle. Once you have released all of your arrows, the asthra power will diminish to a flicker.'

The bow gleamed, begging to be picked up, but when I reached for it, Guru*ji* stopped me.

'First, you must quell your own internal fire,' he said. 'If not, then you act in haste. And haste, boy, is like the wind, which serves only to fan the fire.'

I was still focused on the idea of fighting with fire.

'If fire is your ultimate goal, then how are you any different from a rakshasa?'

Guru*ji*'s words hit hard. The comparison reminded me of Elias snarling the word *terrorist*. Suddenly I felt sick.

The wisened sage pointed his staff towards the bow, 'Indeed, sometimes fire alone can be hot enough to burn the heat of a fever. Are you ready for the Agneyasthra?'

Agneyasthra. Perhaps it was something like a lightsabre from *Star Wars*, a fictional energy weapon that shot out little balls of fire to knock down the enemy.

But Guru*ji* corrected me. 'Bows and arrows, boy,' he said. 'We are a culture that cultivates archery most assiduously.'

Huh? What did archery have to do with the Agneyasthra?

'Spirits my boy, you'll need to keep them high,' the sage said catching my line of thought again. 'If you are to bypass the rightful years of apprenticeship. An *asthra* is a weapon. And *Agneya*, means "of agni", of fire, that is. But remember it is not fire that powers up the weapon.'

I sat upright, as the Ramayana's verses about weaponry came into focus, 'Of course, it wasn't fire, but divine mantras that powered weapons.'

'Your physical weapon is a mere bow and arrow, but only a bow infused with the divine mantras can release the arrow of fire. However, unless it is used in pure self-defence, it can wreak great havoc. This is the power of the Agneyasthra.'

Guru*ji* began to draw an image of himself on his airborne canvas, bestowing Rama and Hanumana with divine mantras. Then the scene shifted to an enormous battleground where both of them wielded flaming weapons at scores of fire-spitting rakshasas. As each fire-arrow struck the core of a rakshasa's heart, it burst into a ball of bright green flames signifying the destruction of demonic energy. The most vicious of rakshasas, with poisoned fangs, reptilian bodies and menacing talons, were quickly consumed by green flames at the hands of Rama and Hanumana.

Then, a thunderclap resounded across the sky, followed by a flash of lightning. Rishi Vishvamitra was outlined in a white light like a white statue set ablaze in a tungsten flame. He stretched his arms out to his knees. The last three fingers of each hand pointed sharply to the earth below, while his thumb and forefinger circled together, joined at the fingertips.

'*Om agneye namah,* I bow down to invoke the power of Lord Agni!'

His lips moved slowly, murmuring Sanskrit verses in a regular meter. As Guru*ji* came to the end of each verse, and before he went on to the next, a thunderclap flashed the light around his profile sending jagged spokes of white energy out into the space around him. Each verse he chanted grew louder.

As his chanting reached a crescendo, a jagged white light reached out from the top of his head. It hovered back and forth in the sky like a lighthouse beam signalling to ships at sea. Then, it lowered to a horizontal plane, orbiting three times around my torso, before coming to rest at the crown of my head.

I sat frozen while the beam slowly encircled my body. The energy from Guru*ji* infused my being like a drop of ink infusing the molecules of litmus paper.

I was certain that my vision would be blinded by the brilliant whiteness of the light, but no! Instead, my senses became heightened. All around me, the forest turned sharp and vibrant—the colours of the leaves, the silhouette of the branches against the night light, the scent of the frangipani blossoms.

'*Om agneye namah*!' he chanted again.

For several moments, we both sat engulfed by the brilliant white light. Then, as Guru*ji* continued to chant, the white changed to the blue light of Brahman Shakti. Vibrations of Brahman energy seeped through the cellular matter at the outer layers of my body, slowly making its way to my very core.

'OM AGNEYE NAMAH!'

This time, his chant echoed through the forest like a powerful storm that was bound to destroy everything in sight.

And then it was done. The light and the thunder vanished. Guru*ji* and I sat in silence, disturbed by nothing but the sound of tree leaves rustling in the breeze.

'The asthra makes you one with the universe.'

Guru*ji*, still seated in a lotus pose, spoke through his mind—his eyes were closed and his lips did not move.

'Infused with Brahman Shakti and the mighty Agneyasthra, things will be different now. Use the weapon sparingly and you shall find what you seek. Start with the lesser, proceed to the greater. But, at all times beware of impulsive use and the asthra's mighty power.'

My body tingled as Guru*ji* disappeared into nothingness leaving in his place, a large bow and a quiver of three arrows that gleamed in the moonlight—one made of bronze, a second of silver and a third of gold. I got up slowly, picked up the quiver of arrows and slung it over my right shoulder. My bow, though cast of iron, felt light as a feather.

Baalchorni

The next morning, my senses were still heightened from the hermit's magic. The activity around me had the clarity and focus of an HD movie—a butterfly flit by my nose, its orange wing pattern standing out in sharp contrast to the green leaves behind it. A furry she-vanara's hand shot into the frame, to shoo the butterfly away from disturbing my sleep.

'Don't worry,' I said, stretching my arms and legs in a big yawn. 'It beats my alarm clock at home.'

The she-vanara smiled and then scampered off to feed her baby. Several others like her were scattered about the tree branches feeding or playing with their young, but Chimpu, Pandu and the others were nowhere in sight. The guys had gone off to search for breakfast—a he-vanara morning ritual.

Not wanting to impinge upon the she-vanaras' domestic time, I thought perhaps I should go look for them.

I followed a line of trees to the clearing where I'd met Guru*ji* the night before.

'Chimpu? Pandu? Where are you?' I called.

A gentle rustling noise answered me from beyond the clearing. At first, I simply took it to be the sound of leaves moving in the breeze, but then it became more pronounced and developed an additional clomping sound with a regular beat. I followed the noise deep into the thicket. Each time I stepped towards it though, it rustled and changed directions, like a game of hide-and-seek.

Was it a scared deer? No, it couldn't be. I listened carefully—on one hand, it clomped like a horse and on the other, it slithered like a snake. Clomp, clomp, clomp. Slither, slither, slither. Clearly it lacked the deftness of a deer, but it seemed too heavy to be a horse. The rustling sound suggested a slithering creature, but given the heavy footsteps, it obviously wasn't a snake. Then the movement stopped, leaving no clue as to the whereabouts of the creature. I moved slowly from one tree to the next but neither a rustle nor a shadow revealed anything.

Recalling my induction into the community of warriors, my one hand went to my bow and the other reached for my quiver of arrows. But which one was I to use?

Guru*ji*'s advice came back to me—'Start with the lesser, proceed to the greater'. Naturally I should go for the bronze arrow.

Still, where was I to aim? I thought about King Dashratha of Ayodhya, Rama's father. The king was a master shooter who seldom failed to aim at his target, using only the sense of sound as his guide.

I strung the arrow to my bow and listened. To deepen my concentration further, I decided to close my eyes. Slowly, I pivoted around in a circle stopping once I sensed darkness over my eyelids.

Then, I opened them to see the ugliest creature imaginable. Bright yellow in colour, it had a nasty female face with bulging eyes and warts. Around her oddly familiar, mean expression flowed serpentine Medusa locks. Her front legs were clubbed and heavy like those of a giantess, but she had no hind legs. Her rear was long, scaly and swished around behind her, like a tail. No doubt this was the cause of the slithering sound I'd heard earlier. All over her yellow body were boils that oozed neon green pus.

Uggh! My mind immediately went to Athena. It wasn't that she looked like her, or at least not at first glance, but there was something about her manner that was so Athena-like. It was unthinkable though that this Medusa could be anything but a rakshasi—a demoness from Ravana's army sent to endanger the lives of vanaras. I froze in my spot as I stared at her loathsome image.

The creature opened her mouth to expose a green warted tongue, it was forked like that of a snake.

'Think you can get me goopeater?' she hissed.

Goopeater! She knew me better than I realised.

Underneath her reptilian voice, I detected an unwelcome familiarity. I had heard this voice many times before. But before I could gather my thoughts, I was distracted by a movement in a tree behind the rakshasi.

Then, I saw something that wrenched my insides—a panic-stricken she-vanara with three babies, perched on a branch within spitting distance of the gruesome creature. Luckily, the rakshasi had not noticed their presence but the mother was obviously scared to bits about her babies. I knew by now that vanaras could not stay still for long, especially the little ones.

One by one, the vanaras also started popping into the tree branches around the clearing. Back from their food gathering ritual, they stood petrified at my chance encounter. Observing the monster, I realised that she fit the description of the self-serving demoness the vanaras had referred to earlier as Baalchorni. As I stood there with my arrow pointed towards her, I imagined them silently championing my warrior stance against her. Moments later, the little vanaras were unable to contain their fright. One of them screeched; the other jumped; the third began to fling his arms back and forth.

'What do we have here,' the rakshasi said, swirling her tongue and spinning around towards the monkey family. 'Baby vanaras! I almost missed them!'

I needed to act.

'Don't even think about it,' I hollered.

The vanaras who had gathered around us broke their silence upon hearing my threat. The trees around the clearing were soon filled with vanara chitter.

The rakshasi turned around to face me with an evil grin.

'And who are you? Protector of the monkeys? Can stupid threats hold back Baalchorni from her prey?'

The vanaras came out of hiding jabbering in both terror and excitement. Baalchorni was thrilled to see the entourage. To her, vanaras assembled together in one place meant one thing—food. A vicious laugh hurtled from her lungs.

'Monkeys everywhere and not one will offer an old visitor a morsel? What does that say about your hospitality?'

'Baalchorni,' one vanara pleaded, 'our tribes have just settled here after a long winter. There are few of us left. Please leave our children alone.'

Baalchorni let out a peal of laughter, 'But they taste so good!'

She thrashed her serpentine tail against the trees, scattering the bark and leaves in all directions. Then, she took three steps forward and one step back, crouching down to prepare for a long jump. Baalchorni leapt towards the baby vanaras. Their mother managed to grab two babies and swing off in the direction of the jungle-gym, but the third baby remained on the tree screeching in fear as the rakshasi's massive body brushed against her.

I swivelled around, pointing my arrow in the direction of the rakshasi. Convinced it was time for release, I drew it tightly against my iron bow. The hermit's words echoed in my head.

'Use the arrows only in self-defence. The Agneyasthra is no meagre firearm.'

Shooting the arrow at this moment would not, strictly speaking, be in self-defence. The rakshasi had not attacked after all, not with anything beyond words.

But then she was a rakshasi, which meant she couldn't be trusted. Who knew what she'd do next? So, I quickly pulled back the arrow, exaggerating the curvature of the vine threading on my cast iron bow. At the count of three, I focused on my target again and then carefully released the arrow, which sailed through the forest clearing in a perfectly streamlined flow. Along the way, it intersected velvet green leaves, flying insects and airborne scents before piercing the rakshasi straight through her heart, and then taking root in a thick tree trunk behind her.

Baalchorni let out an enormous cry that sounded like the scream of a thousand witches. She brandished her tail while the rest of her body stiffened in pain. She heaved her tail one last time before falling to the ground, lifeless. I stood back and watched, pride swelling my insides, waiting for the vanaras to cheer, but then a horrible thing happened.

The tree struck with the bronze arrow burst into flames. Vanaras caught on its branches swung off, some with scorched tails and bottoms.

A throng of vanaras swung forward from their hiding place in the jungle-gym. Pandu and the old leader were among them.

'It's the asthra!' Buddha shouted. 'He doesn't realise its power.'

The vanaras leapt from tree to tree to try and escape the flames. Pandu grabbed the baby vanara who had come close to being caught by Baalchorni and bounced out of the way as the shrubbery around the clearing went up in flames. Within moments, I was surrounded by a circle of fire and the mayhem had shifted focus from—vanaras escaping the rakshasi to vanaras escaping the flames, which leapt at them greedily. Though they were adept at swinging out of the way, it became increasingly hard to know which way to swing as the fire grew out of control, swallowing the shrubbery as if to fuel its appetite for destruction. I was surprisingly unthreatened by the flames but watched with dismay as they hungrily licked the branches of the jungle-gym.

Something tugged at my bow. It was Chimpu.

'Come on,' he said, 'we need to get out of here!'

He pointed to a clear passage through a group of trees still untouched by flames. The vanaras were fleeing through the passage, one helping the other to escape. With no time to think or react, I blindly followed Chimpu.

~

After leaping, running and swinging through what seemed like miles, we arrived at an open ground of rocks and shrubbery. Overcome by fear and exhaustion, the younger vanaras plonked themselves on to the rocks, their mothers comforting them as best as they could.

But I wasn't tired at all. I scanned the open forest and then turned back to glance at the brilliant glow of flames in the distance.

My heart sank like a heavy stone to the depths of the sea. Earlier, I was convinced that my anxiety to kill the rakshasi was borne out of a desire to save the vanaras but at that moment, I realised this wasn't true.

The hermit's voice echoed through the clearing—'Impetuousness does not belie self-defence.'

Impetuousness? A hot rush of indignance rose up my spine.

'That's unfair!' I responded angrily even though Guru*ji* wasn't present. 'I came across a rakshasi and thought it was the perfect opportunity to use the asthra.' I sighed, forcing back the rush of indignance. It was true. I had been hasty, like I had been on the day of Ma's accident.

The onus was on me to mend the situation. But how could I possibly justify to the vanaras that I'd acted to protect them?

Truth is, I'd "reacted to" rather than "acted at" the sight of Athena, even though Guru*ji* had warned me to use the Agneyasthra in self-defence only.

'And what do you make of that?' his voice asked.

'I didn't slow down to think about my fellow beings, like you told me,' I replied sheepishly. 'By setting the forest on fire, I have now destroyed the homes of the fellow beings who I'd actually set out to protect! They're going to have to move to another part of the forest once again.'

'Are you Arya, the Protector?'

Honestly, at that moment it didn't feel like there was any difference between me and the rakshasi, we had both made life incredibly difficult for the vanaras.

Pandu's Injury

I took a deep breath, gathering the courage to speak.

'Vanaras, I am sorry! Destroying your home was really not part of my plan,' I declared.

The vanaras looked at me dismally, although sympathetically.

'We know you were trying to help and what's done is done,' Buddha said raising his right hand in a conciliatory gesture, 'But what I don't understand is why Guru*ji* would give you the Agneyasthra when you are obviously too inexperienced to realise its power.'

'My instructions were to shoot the arrow only in self-defence,' I admitted shamefacedly. 'I was too caught up with killing the rakshasi, I didn't think about the consequences.'

'Buddha's right!' Surayu shrieked, vaulting back and forth over a fallen branch. 'You haven't even been trained.'

His words set off an argument among the rest of the vanaras. Uggh! They clearly weren't comfortable with my use of the Agneyasthra. Chimpu came bounding to the front of the crowd to interject.

'Don't underestimate Guru*ji*,' he said. 'There has to be a reason that he's done it this way.' But his words were greeted with growls and screeches. So he tried again.

'He has a plan, I tell you. Maybe, it's trial by fire!'

Trial by fire. Was this the test for being impulsive? There had to be a reason that Guru*ji* had given me the asthra without proper training. I scanned the scene, half expecting him to appear, at least in voice, but no such luck.

'We've lost our home!' another vanara screeched. 'Again!'

His words pricked me in the heart just like the asthra itself!

'Well, at least we haven't lost people this time,' Chimpu said.

No sooner had he spoken, than a pitiful wail rose from a cluster of vanaras at the rear end of the crowd. They were hunched over a small body.

'What is it?' he asked, alarmed.

I heard shrieks and tail-thumps from the gathering.

'What is it?' I echoed Chimpu, fearing the worst. We rushed over to catch a glimpse of Pandu lying on the grass, clutching his tail. He was trembling. A horrible sensation began to churn my stomach.

'Pandu, what happened?' I asked.

'The lower half of his body is badly burned,' replied Gopu, another vanara. I tried my best not to panic. This was *my* doing!

'Is there medicine?' I asked frantically.

'We are applying sap from the *kumari* plant,' Gopu responded, 'but the burns are too severe. He needs something stronger.'

'What does he need?' I demanded.

Nobody said anything specific but the chitter would not die down.

'Will somebody please tell me what he needs?' I could hear my voice booming through the crowd.

Buddha wrinkled his face and spoke with a resigned sigh, 'He needs Deep Medicine.'

Deep Medicine? What the heck was that? The vanaras shot suspicious glances at each other without speaking.

'What's Deep Medicine?' I asked, flinging my bow and quiver to the ground.

No answer. I couldn't tell whether they were avoiding the reference or whether they were more concerned with applying aloe vera to Pandu's wounds. I glanced around helplessly, begging for some kind of response.

Since nobody seemed willing to talk to me, the Ramayana was my only recourse. I retrieved it from my quiver and opened it forcibly to the chapter in which Lakshmana, Rama's brother had been mortally wounded. It read—

Lakshmana lay on the battlefield after being struck by rakshasas during the Great War against the demons of Lanka. In an endeavour to help him, Hanumana flew towards the Himalayas to procure "Sanjeevani", a plant from which village doctors produced a magical elixir. Hanumana knew that only this stood a chance of saving his life.

'Sanjeevani!' I shouted out to the crowds. A wave of tension slipped away from my body, even as I uttered the name of the plant. 'It's guaranteed to heal.'

The vanaras shook their heads partly in disbelief and partly in denial. I turned to Chimpu and asked, 'What's the deal?'

'There's no such thing,' he responded.

What was he going on about? It was written, right there in my book. 'Of course there is,' I insisted. 'Are we anywhere near the Himalayas?'

'Arya, the mountains have long since been stripped of the medicine.'

'What do you mean?'

Chimpu looked me in the eye with intent. 'Humans have uprooted our healing botanicals for their selfish purposes, there is no naturally occurring elixir left for the creatures of the jungles.'

'What the ...?' But much as I wanted to contemplate the awful truth of his words, there was no time.

'Well, what's the alternative then?' I snapped. Hot tears began streaming down my flushed cheeks. The thought that Pandu might die was just not an option. All this was a freakish reminder of the situation at home with Ma.

'Look, I'm going to save Pandu,' I said. 'I have to, I am an Arya.' How I longed for Ma! How ironic that right at that moment, she too needed an elixir. Which one should I focus on finding first? Her's or Pandu's? A strong rush of fever tingled through my body. If indeed I was Arya, the Protector, then I knew I must save Pandu while I had the chance. This is exactly what Ma would want me to do.

I grabbed Chimpu by his arm.

'Chimpu, what is Deep Medicine? Where can I find it?' I asked.

The disturbed vanara thumped his tail on the ground. 'I do not know exactly. None of us do.'

But I wasn't ready to give up.

'Well then who does?' I asked.

'Only one person,' Chimpu replied, still not allowing hope into his voice.

'Who?'

'The Medicine Woman of the Backwaters.'

'The Backwaters? What's that?'

'It's part of The Wild Woods surrounded by waterfalls and rainbows,' he said.

'Quite far from here,' Buddha added. 'In the southern direction, towards the Dark Side of the forests near Lanka. There in the Backwaters, the Medicine Woman cooks elixirs of all sorts of herbs and roots, powered by the spell of rainbows.'

His description evoked a vision of a day in my distant past when Ma had cooked roots of medicinal plants from our garden for hours over the kitchen stove. A ray of sunlight through the window gently made its way into her cooking pot. I remember the glass pane breaking the sunshine into all seven colours of the rainbow. Had Ma known about the Deep Medicine? Why had she never shared this with me?

The sound of Pandu's whimpering jolted me back to reality. 'Where are these Backwaters?' I asked Chimpu. 'How do I get there?'

'You can't,' Chimpu replied.

'Why not?' I asked.

This time, Chimpu stared at me as though I had two heads.

'The Backwaters lie on the outskirts of the Dark Side, rakshasa territory. It's far too dangerous.'

'I don't care, I have to go if that's what Pandu needs.'

Chimpu looked crestfallen. I grabbed his shoulder and shook it hard.

'Tell me, how do I get there?'

'If you lose your way then ...'

My determination was giving way to frustration. 'Chimpu, HOW do I get there?'

Chimpu was silent at first. Then, he looked around at Pandu and the other homeless vanaras.

'To get to the Backwaters, you need to follow the direction of the *Pushpak Vimana.*'

I scrunched up my face as I recognised the reference to the flying chariot that Ravana had used to carry Sita to Lanka.

How the heck anyone could trace the direction of a flying chariot beat me. How would I choose a particular path and what were the odds it would lead me to the right direction? I scratched my chin perplexed.

'Well, I could probably guess,' Chimpu said, 'but to be honest, my nomadic existence from season to season, thanks to Baalchorni, has completely destroyed my sense of direction and the forest is too thickly wooded to weave through with accuracy.'

Gosh, we could do with some help from Guru*ji*! I sent a plea out to the hermit asking for him to appear but with no such luck. Pandu, in the meantime, let out a feeble grunt. He was too unwell to speak but he raised his paw and pointed to the book in my hands.

'The epic of course!' I said, confident once again. 'It'll definitely have the answer.' I turned to the pages that described Hanumana's Great Leap over the ocean when he went in search of Sita and ran my fingers over the verses until I came to the one I was looking for.

'The mighty and courageous Hanumana roamed as he pleased, the wide open expanse that was the colour of lapis, which appeared like still water.'

'A wide open expanse the colour of lapis?' I said aloud. 'He hadn't reached the ocean yet, so what could that be? A lake perhaps, or a river?'

'No lakes or rivers anywhere around here,' Chimpu said, shrugging his shoulders.

'There is a small stream a few feet ahead,' said Ranga, a vanara. 'Perhaps, that's where you need to go. That's a mere trickle, hardly expansive! No, there is nothing around here except gulmohar trees surrounded by the earth below and sky above.'

Gulmohar trees! For years Ma had talked about the gulmohar tree and its ability to clear the mind. I glanced up at its pink and yellow blossoms, I'd never actually laid eyes on them before, but was tickled pink in my own way, to see they were just as I'd imagined.

'Wait a minute,' I said, an idea forming in my head. I squinted at the sun shining through the blue sky beyond its branches. 'I have it!'

'What do you mean?' Buddha asked.

'The sky. It's a "wide open expanse".'

'But, the sky is not the colour of lapis,' chimed in a confused vanara, Surayu.

'But, it could be, once the sun sets behind the pink and yellow gulmohar blossoms. Look, as it's doing so right now.'

'How do you know what time Hanumana set out to look for Sita?' Chimpu asked, disgruntled. 'The book doesn't say ...'

'Chimpu,' I laughed, suddenly excited. 'All you have to do is stretch your imagination.'

I sensed Guru*ji* smiling at me from behind the gulmohars, so I read the next few lines out loud.

'Hanumana beat the tops of the trees with his chest. Birds, trees and animals, disturbed in their leafy homes, flew out to see what was happening.'

But, the vanaras didn't understand.

'Don't you see it? Hanumana had begun to fly. His chest was hitting tree-tops, scaring birds and animals in the trees because he was making his way through the sky, following the *Pushpak Vimana* with Ravana and Sita in it.'

A flicker of hope gradually dispelled their disbelief as the story began to make sense. The vanaras began to jump up and down and then kiss their tails in excitement.

'I will go with you!' an eager Chimpu said.

'Me too!' said Ranga.

'And I will join too,' came yet another voice.

It took a few moments to get the others on board. Chimpu would accompany me along with Ranga and Raja, two other vanaras who knew the forests best. I looked down at my sick vanara friend and took his paw in my hand, all the while thinking how there were just a few days—hours—left until they pulled the plug on Ma back home.

'Hang in there buddy,' I said. 'You'll be up and running in no time, as soon as I lay my hands on this Deep Medicine.'

Pandu smiled feebly; there wasn't a whole lot else he could do. But as far as I was concerned, he didn't need to worry anymore. I wasn't yet sure how we were going to do it, but I knew that the next time I saw him, I'd have the Deep Medicine with me.

The Medicine Woman

To say that the journey through the dense foliage of the forests was challenging would be a trivialisation of facts. It was like trying to swim through a stormy ocean when the tide is going against you.

'I can't do it!' I yelped when my bow and quiver got caught in the tree branches for the umpteenth time.

'You'll get through it,' Chimpu said. The three vanaras had stopped four times already to untangle me from the banyan roots and creepers that clung to me like long lost friends. I wiped a drop of sweat from my forehead.

It felt like days since I had showered, but the thought was clearly out of the question. We hadn't come across water all day. We stopped for fruit and nut meals along the way. I stared up at the most brilliant array of stars and constellations thinking how it had been just two days since I landed in the Wild Woods, but it seemed like forever.

On the third morning, we set off at the crack of dawn. After another two hours of swinging through the trees, we finally arrived at a stream of flowing water at the edge of a grassy bank. Surrounded by a series of waterfalls, the sun shone through its showers and reflected a multitude of glistening rainbows. Birds and butterflies flitted about, some of them coming to rest on the bands of brilliant colour. Ranga flopped to the ground, exhausted.

'Is this it?' I asked, my eyes fixated on the colours glistening through their watery prisms.

Once again, I recognised the picture postcard surroundings. But from where? As I observed the brilliant panorama of colours around me, it occurred to me that I was looking at the graffiti outside Rainbow grocery. The one I had intentionally destroyed on that fateful day of Ma's accident!

The vanaras slowed down to gaze at the scene with an apprehensive whimper.

'What's the matter?' I asked nudging Chimpu.

'This is the edge,' he replied, rubbing his tail somewhat nervously.

'Of what?'

'Of reason, of safety, of good.'

'Not sure what you mean by that,' I said venturing towards the stream.

'Wait!' Ranga called. 'Don't do that.'

'Why not?' I asked magnetically drawn to the waterfalls.

'Seriously. You have to be careful ...'

But I didn't care about Ranga's warning. I left them behind. I heard Chimpu's call.

'Someone needs to be with him. I'll go, you both stay here and keep watch.'

The sun shone down on the water creating beautiful flecks of white on its surface. Further on, at the edge of the stream, stood a lady dressed in an ivory white sari that reflected the seven hues of the rainbows surrounding her.

She looked absolutely ravishing, like some angel. With perfectly clear skin, rosy cheeks and ebony-coloured hair cascading down to her waist, her lean body appeared to float on the grassy banks. She faced the eastern shore of the stream, her eyes closed and her arms folded in prayer.

'Woven from the silk essence of caterpillars dreaming about their first flight as butterflies,' I said, fixated on the vision of this angel.

'What?' Chimpu asked, scratching his head in confusion.

'Her sari is woven from caterpillar silk,' I explained. A smile emerged from somewhere inside me and slowly made its way across my face.

'How do you know?' Chimpu asked curiously.

'I've seen one before, just like this,' I replied, calmly without shifting my gaze.

A cool luminosity radiated from the lady. She resembled the moon contrasting the blue sky of a sunny day. Her voice began to lilt the familiar words of the Gayatri Mantra, *'Om bhur bhuva svaha...'*

I turned to Chimpu. His face shone with awe. 'That's her, isn't it?'

He nodded.

'That's the Medicine Woman, surrounded by her rainbows.'

I'd never seen anything quite like it.

'Who would imagine that such a magnificent place should exist so close to the rakshasa territory.' Chimpu said.

'What's that?'

'Arya, did you even listen to anything we said on the way? We are now on the outskirts of Lanka!'

Had I listened more carefully to Chimpu's words, I'd have understood why the vanaras were so anxiety-ridden about journeying south. But the lady by the waters had drawn me into some kind of trance.

'Who is she?' I asked out loud. It wasn't so much a question as an expression of wonder.

Chimpu was obviously confused

'The Medicine Woman, I told you!'

'No, I mean I've seen her before.'

'Impossible,' Chimpu said. 'She hasn't stepped out of the Backwaters for centuries.'

'It can't be. Our paths have definitely crossed.'

'You must be dreaming Arya!' Chimpu said, rolling his eyes in annoyance.

But I was sure. She had a distinct spiritual aura, mixed with elements of care and wisdom. It took a fraction of an instant for my subconscious mind to recognise the lyrical familiarity of something I had missed for such a long time. Still, I couldn't pinpoint what.

Drawn to her enigma, I stepped forward and dropped everything on the ground. Chimpu didn't follow me. Who knows why my eyes welled up with tears as I raced towards her like a sprinter aiming for the finish line.

She lifted her lashes to gaze at me with silvery-bronze eyes that quickly turned dark golden or greenish-silver, perhaps. The truth was I couldn't really tell. Her eyes seemed to change colour as I looked into them, and the more I looked, the more intense became their colour, and the more drawn to her I was.

'Arya,' she said, opening her arms to me. 'You've come.'

It was all the invitation I needed. The next moment, I was cocooned in her warmth, sobbing tears of relief and excitement as she gently rocked me in the morning breeze. She didn't say anything, she didn't have to, but even so I sensed I'd arrived at my protected place. San Francisco was a long way away from those forests, but at that moment, I felt like I'd finally come home.

Several moments later, the Medicine Woman released her grip and seated me down beside her on a grassy mound.

'You look well, Arya,' she said. She moved a lock of hair away from my forehead. 'The trials of living are strengthening you.'

Suddenly feeling embarrassed, I pulled away.

'Sorry, I don't know what came over me.'

'You have embarked on a difficult journey, but don't be afraid. Things will become easier in time. They already have.'

'Easy? Nothing's been easy these last few days,' I said.

Why did I feel so totally comfortable with this Medicine Woman?

'You now understand the value of Guru*ji*'s words.' She smiled. 'It becomes easier to do right when you understand where you went wrong.'

'You know Guru*ji*?' I asked. The Medicine Woman nodded.

'And like him, you can read my thoughts. Do you also have the powers of Brahman Shakti?'

'No,' she laughed. 'It's different. I listen to the sounds of the Wild Woods through birdsong.'

'Birdsong?'

'The song of the birds,' she replied. She ran her soft fingers through my hair.

'They sing about the happenings in the forests.'

'You understand birds?'

'Only if I listen with focus,' she answered.

At that moment, a new sensation raced through my body. I was overtaken by an extraordinary happiness that I hadn't experienced in a long, long time. It was completely bizarre, as though I was deriving a new strength from the presence of this Medicine Woman, who I felt like I'd known all my life. I felt compelled to talk about my childhood.

'When I was six years old, my mother took me to the Redwood forest near our home,' I said. 'There was this massive tree there, one that stretched so tall, it was impossible to see its top.'

'This was a young shoot just 4, 000 seasons ago,' she had said. 'But over generations, it has witnessed the fickle mood swings of the forest. Today, it reaches high into the sky while being rooted steadfast to its origin—robust, mature and resistant to the onslaught of hostile elements.'

'How many lifetimes will it take you to become like that tree?' the Medicine Woman asked.

I jerked my hands back, amazed. 'That's exactly what my mother said! How did you know?'

'I listened to your thoughts,' the Medicine Woman said, taking my hand in hers. 'At that time, you probably did not understand what she meant but today it makes sense doesn't it?'

I nodded, aware of a strong, new bark, slowly encasing the immature shoot I'd once been. I admired the aura of the Medicine Woman.

'Why are you so beautiful? You are like the moon that is surrounded by mist on a foggy night?' Who knows what sparked the comment, but it came from someplace deep inside.

She responded with only a hazy smile.

'We *have* met before, haven't we?' I asked, almost pleadingly.

The Medicine Woman's eyes softened into a spectrum of rainbow colours.

'Yes, ' she answered. Her voice was oddly familiar and soothing. 'Somewhere in time.'

My confusion must have been apparent. She gazed into my eyes with an energy that lifted my spirits, I almost felt as though I was floating.

'But, that was different, this is my True Self,' she said.

'What in the world do you mean by that?' I asked.

'The True Self is the eternal state of your soul, the place where you experience pure happiness.'

I had no idea what she meant but it didn't really matter.

'Like I said, somewhere in time it will all make sense.'

Her greenish-silver eyes intensified and then changed colour once again, this time to pinkish bronze. As this happened, I felt even more empowered.

'How do you do that with your eyes?' I asked.

Her answer pierced my soul.

'The eyes of your True Self achieve the real purpose of vision. They are the doorways to the universe, open only to those we truly love.'

Gazing deeper into her eyes, I was blown away by visions of my happier times back in San Francisco, times that had long since been trapped within the dusty layers of my memory.

I saw Pa strolling down the ocean walk on Crissy Field, whistling a tune from his favourite TV show; Ma tending to the tulsi plant in our backyard. I saw myself, a little boy in Golden Gate Park, learning how to do ollies on my skateboard. As my world came alive in her eyes, I ached to be back in the life that I knew and loved.

Seized by the magic of the Medicine Woman, I felt the need to discuss everything with her. Not just about my unexpected journey to the Wild Woods, but also about what had happened in San Francisco: my sad father, the torture I had faced at school. I outlined every detail about those wicked attempts at cheating, and how I had deliberately tried to hurt Ma. I plucked away at the corners of my memory, the details weren't hard to find.

Throughout my babbling, she listened quietly, stroking my hair and caressing my face. She smiled like she knew what I was going to say next.

It wasn't until I'd arrived at the part about meeting Guru*ji* that it occurred to me why I'd come here in the first place. I jumped up and scanned the scene for Chimpu.

'Oh my gosh!' I said. 'How could I forget Pandu?'

'Well said. Your friends await you in the Coconut Grove,' the Medicine Woman said. She pointed to a cluster of palm trees a few yards beyond the stream.

'The Coconut Grove?'

'There you will continue your journey.'

'But what about the Deep Medicine? Can you conjure it with your rainbow spells?'

She sighed.

'All I can do is help you realise its value, Arya. The medicine is already in your hands.'

What? All that was in my hands was my Ramayana, my iron bow and a quiver with two arrows.

The Medicine Woman helped me up and ushered me towards the Coconut Grove, 'Your next step is to find a plant that has no medicinal value.'

The task seemed counter-intuitive but hey, I was up for the challenge. Besides, how much of a challenge could it be? The forest was filled with plants. Only, I had to hurry. Pandu, after all, was in serious pain.

'Wouldn't it be more efficient to choose the rainbow-powered option?'

But the Medicine Woman was adamant.

'Only when you race against time do you stand the chance of losing. Slow down. It's the only way you will find what you need, somewhere in time.'

Somewhere in time. Those words again.

It was not like she left me with much of a choice. I folded my hands in a namaste and took a few steps towards the forest, when I was suddenly stopped by the call of her voice.

'Arya, aren't you forgetting something?' the Medicine Woman called.

She gestured towards my cast iron bow and my quiver, and my Ramayana still sitting comfortably on the mound.

'A warrior never goes anywhere without his defence,' she said.

Oopsey! How scatterbrained was I? And how much overlap there was in what she and Guru*ji* had said. I guess they were both gurus, after all.

The Shape-shifting Rakshasa

Finding the plant shouldn't have been too difficult given the scores of shrubs that existed in the undergrowth of flowering trees. However upon entering the Coconut Grove, it was clear that the Backwaters' landscape was very different to what I'd encountered in other parts of the Wild Woods. There were no gulmohar or amla trees here, just the odd lone Banyan standing tall among coconut palms.

'Chimpu? Ranga? Raja?' I called, looking for my friends. There was no sign of them, but they couldn't be too far.

The grove was so dense that sunlight was scarcely visible, except for when the odd ray found its way through the thick green canopy of palm leaves. I stood in a coconut garden, something that Ma had longed for when she reminisced about her younger days in the coastal regions of India. Despite plenty of palm trees planted throughout the city, San Francisco's urban backyards had no place for coconut palms, at least not the kind that provided fruit or prayer room paraphernalia.

The trees journeyed upwards seeking sunlight through their tops. The forest floor was a carpet of shrubs. Some rose out of the soil on their own, others burgeoned creepers that clung to the tall tree trunks. Tender young coconut fruits that had fallen from the trees lay sprinkled intermittently through the shrubbery and grass. When cracked open, they oozed bright white milk, infusing the grove with the flavour of the tropics.

I picked a fruit and sucked the milk directly through a crack in its shell. Mmmm!

'Chimpu, you've got to try this, it's incredible!' I said.

Completely satiated, I flung the shell into the distance, leaving it to be absorbed by the spongy forest floor.

A rush of leaves behind me signalled Chimpu was swinging into the Coconut Grove on a giant vine.

'What's taking you so long?' he asked irritably. He chomped on a fresh stem of neem, the vanaras customarily used this as a dental aid.

'This enchanted herb garden,' I sighed. 'Being here is taking me to a million places, all in the span of a single afternoon.'

Chimpu's face contorted as the bitterness of the neem oozed from the stem. He closed his eyes and swallowed hard before sinking his teeth into a piece of orange to chase the awful taste away.

'Ranga and Raja are waiting, we have a sick vanara to attend to.'

'Help me then. I need to find a non-medicinal plant.'

'What sense does that make?' Chimpu asked, contorting his face again.

'Are you questioning her magic?' I snapped. 'We need the Deep Medicine don't we?'

'Sorry,' Chimpu replied. 'You're right. Let's get to it.' Something sharp, almost peppery wafted through the air.

'What is that?' I asked, raising my head to sniff at it.

'Tulsi.'

'The miracle plant! An elixir for vitality. Ma's favourite medicinal herb!' I clapped my hands, delighted. 'Wasn't Tulsi a lady, once upon a time?'

Chimpu nodded flicking a fly off of his tail. 'A young girl in Vrindavan, the sacred gardens of Lord Krishna, fell in love with Krishna until Radha, Krishna's eternal consort, laid a curse on her causing her to become a plant. A Vedic household is considered incomplete without a tulsi plant right in the middle of the courtyard. Of course, we don't have that issue in the forest.'

'San Francisco homes don't have courtyards, you know,' I said plucking a tulsi blossom. 'Ma would set ours in an earthen alcove situated in the centre of the family room, to repel bugs that came in from the garden during late summer.'

I broke off the flowers as I had seen her do so often and squeezed out their essence onto the tips off my fingers.

'Whatever!' Chimpu said, mildly annoyed. 'It's clearly medicinal. What else do we have?' I rummaged around for several moments before unearthing a tough, fibrous root with a distinctively meat-like aroma.

'*Ashwagandha*!' Chimpu exclaimed. 'Named after the virility of the horse.'

'That's the Indian ginseng! It is an exotic Indian herb that has amazing stress-relieving properties among other things,' I said.

'Not sure what that is,' Chimpu said wrinkling his nose. 'But this one is *tough, tough, tough*! The only way to make it palatable is by boiling and stirring it with other herbs and medicines for hours, but once you've done that you have the essential food for strength, virility and physical power.'

'Well, if that doesn't sound like Deep Medicine then I don't know what does!' I said, frustrated.

Something caressed the back of my neck. This one I knew already. *Pushpalata,* a creeper of pink flowers that blossomed only by the touch of female hands. It always reminded Ma of her own mother, Pushpa.

'The black vine is filled with bright pink blossoms. A lady has obviously been here recently,' Chimpu said. 'Probably the Medicine Woman herself.'

Chimpu identified every plant and its unique healing quality.

'They are all medicinal as far as I can tell,' Chimpu said. By now he was getting quite impatient.

Just then something rustled through the leaves. Chimpu turned towards the direction of the sound, his muscles all tensed up.

A moment later he relaxed as Ranga and Raja emerged through the foliage, both clearly agitated. 'What's happening?' Ranga asked. 'We don't have all the time in the world, you know.'

Before either of us could answer, we heard another rush of leaves behind Ranga, this time accompanied by a faint patter.

Something was on the prowl. All three vanaras grew tense this time. Chimpu lifted his finger to his lips.

My hands immediately went to my quiver. I quickly pulled out my silver arrow, strung it to my bow and listened closely, trying to gauge the quality of the sound. The last time this happened, the culprit was Baalchorni but this sound was different. It suggested a light-footed creature, deft and fleet. Quiet as a mouse, Ranga waved his arms over his head in a silent signal to catch our attention. When all eyes were turned his way, he pointed to a place about six feet in front of my arrow. Two large eyes and two pricked up ears stared at us. The animal's face would have been totally camouflaged had it not been for a telltale crimson flower that stood out in contrast to its golden skin.

'It's a chinkara!' I whispered, instantly recognising the spotted deer, native to the forests of India.

I loved all animals, but had a soft spot for deer, perhaps because they roamed freely through the Northern California landscape. Often while skating through the national parks of Marin or in the Presidio, I'd chance upon a grazing deer. But not chinkara. These I'd only seen in the zoo and in the wildlife magazine *Sanctuary*.

I lowered my bow and placed the silver arrow back in my quiver. The two vanaras closely observed the deer, which headed closer to the group. It didn't have antlers, a sign that it was female.

'A young fawn who's lost her way,' I said. 'She's probably looking for her mother.'

The fawn began to move through the trees. I took a few steps after her.

'Arya, no!' Chimpu warned. His stern tone was quiet, yet, underscored by fear.

But I didn't listen.

The vanaras began to chitter nervously but this time they tried to contain their voices. Raising alarm outside rakshasa territory was not a good idea.

'Arya, what are you doing?' Chimpu asked.

Alarmed by his voice, the fawn leapt away from the crowd.

I shot an annoyed glance at the vanara. Then, I followed the fawn's tracks.

'You have to stop him!' I heard Ranga tell Chimpu. He was beating his tail violently against a branch, a sure sign he was concerned.

The chinkara sprang forward leading us all through the wild grass.

Although speedy in her step, she didn't seem like she was in a particular hurry, at least not at first. Every once in a while though, she'd stop and look around for something, whimpering loudly as she did so. I kept pace with her all the way and before long we were both well ahead of the vanaras. Then, as though responding to an alarm call, the chinkara suddenly began to make sharp movements with her head and she quickened her pace.

'She's more upset now than she was before,' I heard Chimpu shout. I detected apprehension in his voice.

'Maybe, she's been looking for her mother for a long time,' Raja said. I turned around slightly to see Chimpu out of the corner of my eye. He was twitching uncontrollably.

'No. Something's not right. She doesn't appear to be the type of animal that would be in need of a mother,' he said.

Yeah? What kind of judgement call was that? I recalled a conversation between Ranga and Raja earlier in the day when they had talked about how Chimpu was well respected for his sixth sense, especially when it came to the forest creatures.

'It always comes to good use when the pack goes hunting for food,' Ranga had said.

Still, he couldn't be right about this fawn. She was definitely distraught, her whimpering grew frantic as she picked up speed.

Chimpu tried to get my attention.

'Arya, stop. We need to get back to the medicinal plants.'

But I paid no attention, I was totally bewitched by the fawn.

As we wove through the forest, following at her heels, the landscape went through a complete transformation. The tree cover became denser and the foliage multiplied, completely blocking all light from the sky. The forest was now dark as night. The coconut palms disappeared, giving way to a thicket of stumpy trees whose grey-brown roots resembled old and ugly faces. Deeper into the thicket, the faces on the tree trunks contorted in anger. Their leaves were no longer soft or velvety like those I'd seen before, instead, they were jagged and spiked with infectious looking thorns that stood out from their branches. A gusty wind began to howl tunes of painful agony.

The vanaras were now screeching at the top of their lungs, but the sound of their anxiety was muffled by the ferocity of the wind. The fawn also changed, her pace quickened to a gallop as we moved through the foliage; she was clearly aware of us shadowing her. Unlike before, she now seemed not in the least bit threatened by our voices. When she turned to glance at the vanaras, her eyes had metamorphosed from soft brown to flaming red.

'It isn't a deer at all!' Chimpu squealed. 'We've been following a shape-shifting rakshasa!'

Raja began to yelp incomprehensibly.

'Arya!' Chimpu hollered.

'Arya,' Ranga squealed, 'What about the healing plant?'

I heard the question but couldn't answer. Even though I was startled by the eyes of the fawn, she had me under a spell. I was too captivated by her to stop.

'Arya!' Chimpu called again. 'The plant!'

'Later!' I responded through the thick of my trance.

Then, a strange sensation emerged from deep in my core. It started out like a bundle of energy but no sooner did it begin to surge upwards through the centre of my being, than it became obstructed by thoughts of the fawn. The stream of would-be energy then curdled inside my body's energy channels creating a lump that wouldn't move. Like a stone stuck in a narrow tunnel. I stopped for a moment to think about the sensation, but fearing I'd lose her, I pushed the feeling away and continued with my pursuit. The creepers with brilliant coloured flowers had long given way to a winding passage of jet black vines. An unpleasant, stale food-like odour substituted the aroma of tropical spices that had scented the air when we first saw the fawn. It intensified as we progressed on our way through the thorny vines.

By now the vanaras were incredibly distressed. Leaping forward to catch up with me, they screeched relentlessly and gestured frantically to stop me from going deeper into the brambles.

'Arya!' Ranga yelled. He wrapped his tail around my waist while holding on to a sturdy tree branch. Raja followed suit.

'Wake up,' Chimpu cried, waving his arms desperately as his tail swung to and fro in my face. 'You've got to snap out of it. SNAP OUT OF IT NOW.'

The lump of stuck energy throbbed inside my chest each time the vanaras spoke. It vibrated like an alarm bell, alerting me of something bad. Better sense told me that my friends were right, that they were concerned about my safety but I couldn't understand why I struggled to ignore their warning signs, or why my attraction to that chinkara was so intense that it amplified some dormant physical strength enabling me to shake free of Ranga's grasp. With the power of a thunderbolt, I sped towards her, leaving the vanaras chittering way, way behind.

I could no longer see the fawn clearly. For a while, I relied on her silhouette as she leapt through the foliage, but then when it became too dark even for that, I followed the sounds of her movement. Then, a macabre transformation jolted my bones out of my skin. My trance was suddenly broken when the fawn's silhouette transmutated into that of a menacing ogre with huge talons. The chinkara vanished into thin air.

'Ouch!' I cried as something sharp pricked my left side. I found myself blindly grappling with thorny vines that had wrapped themselves around my extremities, like the sticky web of a black widow spider. In a flash, I came to my senses.

'Chimpu? Ranga? Raja?' I called out, looking around frantically for my friends. But I'd left them behind long ago. I was all alone in this menacing jungle, my mind a flurry of questions. Where were the vanaras? Had they stopped in better judgement? If so, then why had they not stopped me too? But they had. They had tried to stop me. Suddenly shocked at what had transpired over the last several minutes—hours—who knew how long, I recalled the vanaras' call—

'Arya, stop. You cannot trust the fawn. She's headed to the Dark Side.'

The Dark Side. Back in the jungle-gym, the vanaras had used the term to describe Lanka, the dreaded home of Ravana and the rakshasas. The name had caused them to clap their fists on their chests—the vanara war cry, sounded only during times of emergency, signalling the onslaught of the enemy. Here in the ugly part of the forest, I'd turned a deaf ear to their warning, following my vision single-mindedly. And now, that vision had led me to a spider's web.

I yanked at the suffocating vines but each time I freed myself from a chain of vines, another seemed to find its way around me, pulling me tighter than before. My bow and arrows were rendered utterly useless. What I needed was a knife or a sword, but where was I to get one? The wind had picked up and was wailing through the thicket like black-robed hags mourning the death of a witch. I looked around me but couldn't even tell the way back to the Coconut Grove.

My mind wandered back to the Ramayana nestled safely in my quiver. I couldn't help thinking how my story was eerily like Rama's. He too had been lured into the forests by a shape-shifting rakshasa in the guise of a deer who led his world into a trap. The vanaras had seen this all along. Why hadn't I? How could I have been so colossally stupid?

The lump of energy in my chest had turned cold and hard. It blocked all sensation of the outside world forcing me to focus on the value of Rama's story. The message was right there all along but I hadn't paid any attention. Once again, I'd been blinded by my own pursuit, rather than adhering to the all-important task I'd set out for—to save Pandu.

'Ravana!' I shouted into the howling wind. 'I get it now. I know why you want to destroy the Ramayana! It's not just a desire to erase history, you want to eradicate the healing capacity of the Ramayana, so everyone is forced to live in your stupid rakshasa-infested world!'

A vine strangled my face as if to obstruct my mouth from speaking. But I resisted.

'Well, I've got news for you, Ravana! The medicine's been in my hands all along. It's up to me to tap into it, and tap into it, I will!'

I closed my eyes to shut out the evil around me. As the wind and the trees twisted my body in their terrifying grip, I knew it was time to tap into my Brahman Shakti.

I focused hard on the inner depths of my body, until I found an energy tunnel taking shape within me. It advanced through my centre and emerged through the crown of my head. Where was the energy? I searched for it, drawing down into the earth, through water, fire, air and all the elements that comprised my being. My mind's eye dug deeper and deeper into the tunnel until I reached the spot that I had been looking for—my root, the storehouse of Brahman Shakti. It was my bedrock, vital with the glow of creative energy.

I called upon my storehouse to release its blue energy of creation similar to what I'd seen flowing from Guru*ji*'s staff. The embers of Brahman Shakti responded to my call by gradually becoming fuller and more pronounced until they coagulated into a potent ball that burst upwards through my central tunnel, and erupted through the crown of my head into a lava flow of brilliant blue energy that shook the sinister vines and trees right to their core, forcing them to release their hold on me completely.

I heard the sage's voice—'A path can be revealed only to he who shall seek it.'

I opened my eyes to a path that had been formed by a separation of the sinister trees before me. It started right from where I stood; here was my chance to follow my own path, something I should have done a long time ago rather than going after the trickster chinkara.

Tightening my grip on my quiver of arrows, my bow and my Ramayana, I began to stride forward. It was horribly dark as night had taken over. The wind was still howling but I focused on the path. Wherever it wound, a faint white glow cast by a misty moon on a foggy night, guided me forward. I couldn't see where the moonlight came from but I knew I didn't have to run anymore.

The Army of Rakshasas

The forest was a chamber of evil. The gusty wind howled like a cyclone of witches that had cast me into murky darkness. Who knew that the land of the Ramayana could be this sinister? Had Rama also contended with the forces of the night?

I was grateful for one blessing—the path ahead was perfectly carved out by the faint white glow of the moon. Nasty looking trees bent towards me on either side but the moonlight seemed to exert a silent force, obstructing them from crossing over to cause harm.

Slowly but surely, I edged forward but then when I least expected it, I lost my footing. The land fell sharply away from my feet causing me to tumble into a heap of mud on the slope of what appeared to be a steep hill. I stood up cautiously, shook off the mud and slowly put my right foot forward. As soon as I made contact with the ground, I put my left foot forward, cautiously. I continued this way for a few more strides, but suddenly found to my horror, that there was no ground beneath my feet. My foot hovered in the air for a few moments, before I settled it back on the ground.

I opened my eyes as wide as possible and then squinted for the sharpest vision I could muster. But I could see no more than two-feet of blackness. Where was I to go from here?

As if to answer my question, the moonlight moved a few feet forward into the blackness, ushering me on to a path that continued straight. In complete contrast, a gust of howling wind thrust upon me from behind, and steered me towards the right. The elements were working in opposition now, each indicating a different way forward. Which way was I to follow? The moonlight that had gotten me out of my last entanglement, or this gust of wind that had suddenly showed up, promising new hope and direction?

It had been Guru*ji*'s intention that I become a warrior worthy of wielding the Agneyasthra and arguably by that time, I was well on my way. But what I couldn't comprehend then was that I still lacked trust and discipline, the marks of a true warrior. Later, I would remember that moment and kick myself for not following the path indicated by the moonlight, but at that time, I had lost trust in its protection. Following the gust of wind seemed perfectly justifiable. Only moments ago my own feet had been walking on air and more than anything, I was haunted by that old, insecure dream of falling into emptiness.

So I swerved to the right, and instantly regretted my decision as I advanced into nothingness. Without the moonlight as my guide, I began rolling down the unyielding ground, completely losing my control. Gasping for air, I reached out but found nothing to grasp on to. No plant, no reed, no thorny bush. The rigid stone of the hillside scraped against my skin as I tossed and turned downwards.

Finally, the land flattened out, bringing me to rest. My body ached slightly, yet I remained unharmed, protected perhaps by the Brahman Shakti that I had recently tapped into. Reaching for my weapons to ensure they were still tightly wound to my body, I was relieved to find them safe.

Then, the howling of the winds gave way to a muffled noise. At first, it sounded like the purring of cats in the distance. But soon the purring increased. It resembled the murmur of engines whirring in an airfield. I strained my neck to make sense of what was happening. Although I couldn't see clearly, I figured that the noise was coming from somewhere behind, and also from above. How strange! The sound increased once again and I heard the thunderous clap of a lightning cloud.

A flash of lightning changed the visual landscape. The moonlight shone upon a wide expanse, illuminating the scenery. I detected a massive army of boulders spinning down the steep hillside above me. The noise of the boulders elevated as they slowly gathered speed in my direction.

Astounded by the sight of the advancing avalanche, I rooted myself to the ground. Terror tingled every nerve ending in my body, before numbing all sensation. So, I lay there crouched in the path of danger, wondering what could be more dreadful—death itself, or its terrifying approach.

Something compelled me to glance up at the moonlight. The misty white light coalesced into a silhouetted image of the Medicine Woman.

Of course, the glow was her protection! This is why I should have trusted it all along.

Her voice echoed into the darkness, 'The medicine is in your hands; I can only help you realise its value.'

Why was it that I always took a step too late? How had Rama dealt with the idea of impending death? I pulled the Ramayana from my quiver. The pages no longer fluttered open by the book's own magic, I was in complete control. I opened it to the part which recorded the final years of Rama's life.

'When the king had fulfilled his earthly duties, a messenger sent by the gods appeared to inform Rama that the mission of his incarnation was over.'

I processed the words in my head. Rama had willingly gone to the arms of death, accepting that his life's purpose was well served. It was perhaps the ideal situation but could the same be said of me, a boy who now hovered in death's path, only after living a life of pain?

The Medicine Woman spoke again in the darkness. In her voice, I heard the lyrical undertones of my mother. 'Death delivers us into the sunlit fields of happiness. In the twilight, before one reaches that sunlight, a dying person comes face to face with the scenes of his life, his loved ones, his lost ones, and all the karmic episodes that have brought him to this threshold.'

'Ma, is it time?' I asked. But there was no answer. I knew then it wasn't my moment to die. Creative energy from deep inside my being began to take shape once again. As my senses sharpened, I saw that the boulders advancing at me down the hill were not boulders at all. Instead, they appeared to be rakshasas, an entire army of them, charging at me like depraved animals set loose after years of captivity.

Hundreds, maybe thousands of hoofed monsters raced down the hill, spitting green fire from their nostrils. Some were reptilian creatures with brown liquid oozing from their pores and craters dotting their hideous scaly skin. Others possessed seemingly human forms, but their eyes gleamed with vengeful fire. There were some that were half man, half-animal, but their menacing presence showed that they were wholly demons. Their forked tongues hung down from open mouths, revealing razor-sharp fangs gnashing of their own accord.

It wasn't the first time I'd looked into the face of evil but never had I been presented before an entire army of demons. Obviously, Ravana's quest for the last copy of the Ramayana had led them to me and here in the rakshasa territory, they had the advantage. But I knew one thing—the potential of Brahman Shakti could far outweigh the rakshasa energy. Every verse of the book in my hands was written on the basis of this underlying truth.

Abiding by my strong sense of awareness seemed the most opportune thing to do. So, I closed the book and placed it safely back in my quiver. I listened to the rakshasa hooves beat against the rock in a single thud each time they advanced a few feet forward. I inhaled. Even at a distance of several feet, the odour of the toxic fumes snorted out through their nostrils was overwhelming. Reacting in haste had not been the concern this time, but I knew I was moments away from being crushed in a stampede if I didn't act. So, I took a calculated decision.

I whipped out my silver arrow and strung it to my bow. Taking a deep breath, I centred myself, drawing energy from my root yet again. I had one arrow to defend myself against the onslaught of an entire army.

I closed my eyes.

I paused for several moments, my senses opened to the task at hand. Blocking out the sound of approaching doom, I waited for my signal. When the blue energy drew up through the tunnel at the centre of my being, I sent a silent prayer into the night sky and released my silver arrow.

As it skimmed through the space between me and the avalanche of rakshasas, everything else lingered in slow motion. Dust was kicked up from the earth by the rakshasas' hooves, its particles were suspended in the air, and the leaves displaced from the surrounding trees broke into a lazy dance without actually hitting the ground. As the arrow moved forward, the army of approaching rakshasas crippled before my eyes. When the arrowhead pierced the core of the army, the force of the Agneyasthra came alive once again setting its target on fire with a massive explosion. It detonated the avalanche with an enormous discharge of fire, scattering the rakshasas in every direction.

I watched the brilliant sound-and-light show of howling demons as they were vanquished by fire. The night sky was splintered by virulent flames that greeted one another with a thunderous ovation. Balls of fire pervaded the blackness around me, like shooting stars across the wide expanse of the universe. Each time one ball of fire stumbled upon another in the darkness, the friction would release a bolt of lightning, further trailed by a retinue of shimmering fire-dust. The sky was thick with smoke.

~

I recalled the words of Guru*ji* as I watched the darkness transform to a familiar night sky lit by a full moon—*This is no meagre firearm.* This time however, the moonlight was cast wide, allowing me to see clearly for miles. Its silvery-white glow was enhanced by a blanket of burnt sienna, left over from the embers of the exploding rock.

I had come to rest on a crag jutting out from the cliff. What could possibly have cushioned this long fall? The cliff wall rose steeply all around, its rim surrounded by thick, dense forest. Even in the daylight, I couldn't have imagined walking through the forest in which the dense trees ended so abruptly, leading to a deep canyon of darkness.

Something shifted on the ground next to me. My quiver began to slide over loose gravel. My golden arrow. My lifeline. I jerked forward to catch it, but so intent was I on rescuing the arrow from the abyss that I forgot the other most important thing in the quiver, the Ramayana.

It took a fraction of a second for the book to slip out and fall into the darkness. Then, like a spring fairy, it floated through the air before sinking into the canyon. A moment later, it had completely disappeared.

An unrecognisable sensation pulsed through my body—neither heat nor cold, neither weakness nor strength, neither hunger nor thirst, neither pain nor comfort. Just a hollow sensation. Maybe this was the beginning of my end. Maybe if I closed my eyes I would see the twilight.

Levitating over Lanka

A familiar voice rang in the shadow of the night air. 'Not the twilight.'

I opened my eyes to Rishi Vishvamitra, suspended in the sky in front of me. He was seated with his legs crossed one over the other, counting his rudraksha beads with his eyes closed. Below him, lay the depths of the canyon. He was levitating, something that could be done only with the deepest concentration. How then could he possibly talk at the same time?

There was something about him that was different than before but I couldn't put my finger on it. Guru*ji* continued with determination in his voice.

'You have places to go boy before you ever enter the threshold of twilight.'

Then, Guru*ji* opened his eyes.

'Consider this an interlude. A brief respite, where you can catch your breath before you proceed to your final ordeal.'

'You mean we're not done yet?'

Guru*ji* stopped counting.

'Must I answer a question with another question?'

Which meant, there was certainly more to go through. Sure, it made sense—I still had a golden arrow after all.

And the Ramayana, I had no choice but to retrieve it. Still, how?

It occurred to me that although Guru*ji*'s language still maintained its less than straightforward style, he was no longer speaking in riddles.

'Boy, I speak in the manner I have always spoken. It is you who has changed your perception. At this point in your journey you understand the rhythm of not only my words, but also of how you must proceed.'

It was true. I'd come to understand a lot in the last three days—that vanaras were real but that they lived in danger; that weapons must be used only in self-defence; that one must implicitly trust the counsel of those who offer protection. I'd grown to understand the meaning of the Ramayana. Most importantly, the fact that Ravana had risen and was waiting to get his hands on the last surviving copy of my epic was clear evidence that the battle of good versus evil had no beginning and no end. As Ma had said, the two forces always coexist to maintain balance in the universe.

I saw the scenes of the Ramayana play out in Guru*ji*'s changing eyes—Ravana terrorising the inhabitants of the forest. Ravana in disguise, abducting Sita. Rama defeating Ravana in battle. It all made perfect sense. 'Good' in the guise of Rama had conquered 'evil' in the guise of Ravana, allowing peace to exist for a long period of time. However, the forces of evil had finally risen, as they inevitably do, begging for good to once again play its hand.

'An Arya like Rama is born to humanity each time the scale is tipped over by the weight of evil,' the Guru*ji* said.

I nodded. For the first time ever, I understood why I'd been named Arya, and why I'd come to the land of the Ramayana. As Protector, I was the key to the epic's survival, but the epic was the key to my survival too. This was the reason Ma had weaned me on its stories from my very early days.

Who knew what the final outcome would be? When you fought a battle, any battle, strength could only be achieved in numbers. At any cost, I knew I must reconnect with the vanaras to build my army.

'They have arrived at your side,' Guru*ji* said.

I looked at him blankly. I saw nothing.

'Step out, boy, and then look. You will see clearly only when you separate yourself from the situation that traps you.'

'Guru*ji*, I am seated at the edge of a cliff,' I said. 'To where should I step? I can't levitate like you.'

Guru*ji* smiled at me while counting his rudraksha beads.

'Did it cross your mind to try?' he asked.

It hadn't. Who, with a sane mind, would venture to step out onto a platform of nothing but air? But by then I also knew that Guru*ji* didn't utter words without reason. Although, his challenges were always confusing at first, each time, I came out learning something new.

So I took a deep breath and stepped towards Guru*ji*. A gentle breeze floated me upwards, away from the rocky platform and out into the thin air. When I turned to look back, I saw a throng of vanaras perched on the cliffs above, staring down at the rocky ledge that I had just stepped away from. As if in a dream, I saw that I'd stepped away not just from the ledge, but from my own body, which lay motionless. Chimpu, Ranga and Raja, stood immediately peering over, concerned for my life.

'How can it be?' I asked in amazement.

'As I said, only when you separate yourself from your predicament, can you see the whole truth.'

The edges of Guru*ji*'s mouth curled up into the hint of a smile.

I totally got it! What had seemed like an impossible task before was so perfectly logical and clear now.

'Guru*ji*, what about the Ramayana?'

'You passed it on to the grip of those who wanted it.'

A familiar lump of stuck energy pounded in my chest.

'Look below,' Guru*ji* said. 'See for yourself.'

I did as he said and peered over my cushion of air. Down below was a bird's-eye view of a startling and heinous sight. I was no longer peering at a vast expanse of nothing, but rather into an ominous canyon swarming with sinister rakshasas of every shape and form. Large ones, small ones, horned ones and winged ones. Some had a single eye that protruded erect above a sharp central tusk, similar to that of cyclops. Some with massive wings and webbed limbs flew through the lower depths of the canyon like giant bats, protecting the mouth of the canyon from intruders.

I'd never seen anything like it before. Directly beneath me, three long-beaked creatures that looked like carrion birds flew round and around, opening their jaws as they completed each circle, to reveal thick ugly fangs that reeked with poison. Farther below, I saw snake-like creatures slithering on scale-covered bellies. In some ways, they resembled the reptilian monsters of the night before but they had no hoofed legs to gallop on. Instead, they writhed about in the depths of the canyon flitting their forked tongues towards the sky.

There were creatures with tentacles and human-like upper bodies. Each inch of skin was concealed by bright, red pus-filled pimples. Other rakshasas had the bodies of men, but instead of hair, their heads and extremities were blanketed by thorny feathers. Each rakshasa snorted toxic green fumes from its nostrils, mouth or snout. There were thousands of them, spitting, hissing, cursing. Each looked more menacing than the last.

In the light of the morning, their features were much more clearly discernable than those of the rakshasa army the night before. These beasts had venomous expressions indicating greed, hunger and carnage. Their eyes were big, angry and red like volcanic craters. I'd seen these eyes before, first in Baalchorni, and then in the chinkara. How could I not have known? It was so obvious, looking at them now, that the fawn had been a shape-shifting rakshasa, luring me to this pit of hell. Part of Ravana's master plan to draw me here and extract the book from my grasp.

Underneath the demons, the fetid moss floor of the canyon undulated like a living carpet. There were holes situated all over the floor erupting a dark grey liquid that was foul both in smell and consistency, like industrial waste from a factory silo. There were neither plants, nor water in the canyon. Only thick piles of bones or flesh, victims of the carnage were brought here from somewhere else. I shuddered. If rakshasa territory looked like this from above the ground, then what could the netherworld possibly look like?

I'd never imagined that rakshasas of this sort still lived, except in Lanka. But, I knew from the Ramayana that Lanka lay across an expanse of ocean at the southern tip of the Indian subcontinent. Was this the Dark Side? It couldn't be Lanka. I hadn't crossed an ocean.

'Have you forgotten that you came from San Francisco?' Guru*ji* asked.

I looked at him, perplexed.

'But, I fell through a fault.'

Guru*ji* laughed.

'Like I said before, sometimes you have to fall through a fault.'

Guru*ji* stroked his beard. 'Each person has his own Lanka, boy, where he must fight his own demons if he is a true warrior. This one is yours, you have already crossed oceans of peril to get here.'

Wow! Guru*ji*'s words had seemed like muddled sentences during our early encounters, but now they came sharply into focus.

'How do you propose to get out of your Lanka?' Guru*ji* asked. 'And how will you complete your task?'

He pointed to a cushion of animal bones with incandescent green flames licking its edges. On it lay my Ramayana. Ugghh!

'Indeed,' Guru*ji* continued. 'Your epic has been strategically placed on none other than Ravana's throne.

I sensed the light of the early morning behind my eyelids and heard the twittering of birds. It took me back to a verse about the origins of the Ramayana—

'One morning in ancient India, Rishi Valmiki chanced upon the conversation of two birds. Their lilting melody sang about the travels of Rama.'

Birdsong! The Medicine Woman had referred to it. Humans had evolved, yet most of them had lost the capacity to understand the melodies of Mother Nature. I listened with rapt attention.

'A boy woke up to complete his journey,' the birds sang. 'For he had realised the meaning of his name.'

The birdsong was interrupted by the call of a wild animal echoing through the early morning air. I couldn't tell what it was, but it had a distinctly feline quality.

Then, I heard the familiar sound of chittering. My eyelids fluttered several times before opening to the sight of three vanaras peering down at me.

'He's alive,' I heard Chimpu say. '*Jai* Rama, he is alive after all!'

The Dark Side

As the trio of vanaras stared down into my face, I felt like I'd woken up out of a coma and was now being examined by a dentist and his assistants. Their happy expressions made it clear that they were relieved to see me alive. Chimpu's tail twitched nervously though, from side to side.

'Arya,' he said. 'Can you see me?'

I grunted in response.

'Bring him to his senses,' I heard Ranga say. 'Make him sneeze.'

A moment later, one of the vanaras began to tickle my nostrils with a thin blade of grass.

AAAtichoooo!

I sprang up in an instant. The vanaras began to clap and jump for joy.

'I'm sorry,' I said sheepishly recalling the chinkara chase. 'I let you down again, didn't I?'

'Not to worry,' Chimpu said. 'If we vanaras hadn't made mistakes repeatedly, we wouldn't be in danger of going extinct. But now that you're awake and hopefully past your deer fixation, it is time to plan our strategy.'

'Strategy?'

'Ravana is about to burn your copy of the Ramayana. If he does that, it will be the end of us all.'

Of course. My levitation experience came back to me, I recalled everything I'd seen in the canyon.

'We've gathered an army to help you,' Chimpu said.

I heard a shrill noise from the far side of the mountain. It was the screeching sound of the vanaras. Of course, their hair stood on end at the slightest mention of 'The Dark Side', but even so, the cliff edges were now covered with scores of vanaras ready to fight the demons. With them were hundreds of monkeys swinging, loping and leaping. It was a vanara sena, an army of my very own! Who'd have imagined?

'At your service, Arya,' Chimpu said. 'We're all ready.'

I blinked my eyes. How could this possibly be efficient without Hanumana in the lead?

'Chimpu, what about weapons?' I asked.

'We have none,' he replied. 'When Ravana subsided to the depths of the earth, the vanaras were overjoyed to have gained freedom from his tyranny. We laid down our weapons for good. We never imagined that the rakshasas would resurface from the dark quarters, sooner than later.'

The difference between Rama's army and mine glared me in the face—my soldiers had no weapons. How was this ever going to work?

'Perhaps we should call upon Rishi Vishvamitra,' I suggested.

But Chimpu wasn't convinced it would help.

'If weapons of any kind were available, Guru*ji* would have made sure that we had access to them ages ago. Besides, times have changed. Look around you, Arya. What do you see? Not vanaras, but monkeys of a lower pecking order.'

He was right. The monkeys outnumbered the vanaras by far.

'Our clansmen had once outshone the other monkey tribes not just in valour but also in numbers. But today, our multitudes are nothing compared to that of our cousins. We must show them solidarity in return for their support. They aren't equipped to use sophisticated weapons of the human kind. We must respect their abilities by abstaining from the use of such weapons too.'

'But how can we possibly outdo these rakshasas? How will we ever get to that bonfire without them tearing us to shreds first?'

'Weapons can be created of sticks, stones and monkey-slings.'

Chimpu offered his advice with a weak smile.

The idea of monkey-slings conjured images of monkeys playing tricks at a zoo, not a formidable army of soldiers.

'We'll have to get deep into the canyon,' Chimpu said, with a newfound determination in his voice. 'Once we do so, we can use sticks and stones to distract the rakshasas.'

'Distract them from what?' I asked.

'From you. Our slinging will annoy them enough to avert their focus. The good thing is that the rakshasas are generally slower to react than monkeys.'

So a perfect strategy could not be planned by this particular army but I could count on their ability to annoy and distract the rakshasas with monkey games.

'Once we have their attention, you will be free to wield your weapon.'

'Chimpu, I have just one arrow left. There are hundreds of rakshasas down there.'

'Arya,' Chimpu said suddenly looking very serious, 'I may not know the art of warfare but I do know this—it's no ordinary weapon that Guru*ji* has given you, it's the Agneyasthra! What's more, your last arrow is golden. It is more powerful than the bronze and silver you were given for practice.'

'Practice? All that was for practice?'

Chimpu nodded. 'You have to trust Guru*ji*, he knows what he is doing.'

He was right. The bronze arrow that I'd shot at Baalchorni, set an entire section of the forest ablaze. Then, the silver arrow caused an avalanche. The golden arrow gleamed when it emerged from the quiver, even in the absence of sunlight. What strength could it possibly hold compared to the others? One thing I knew for sure—it was my last chance, I had to use it wisely.

As I reflected on the power of the arrow, the three vanaras continued to discuss their strategy.

'Given our inferior position, there is no way we can rush into the canyon without a concrete plan,' Raja said.

Chimpu agreed. 'We will enter from the far side, which slopes down towards the central valley, and is still thickly wooded. But how to approach?'

That there was even a "far side" was news to me. But, the approach was quite clear in my head. They should simply use the hidden warfare approach that I'd learned about recently from watching a school production of a Shakespeare play about a king called Macbeth.

Chimpu was immediately curious. 'How does that approach work?' he asked.

'You camouflage your presence with tree stumps,' I replied. 'The rakshasas will just assume that you are trees. Then, little by little, you begin descending on the hillside carrying the tree stumps. By evening you should reach the edges of the Dark Side but all the rakshasas would see are trees.'

'Aren't the rakshasas going to wonder how the trees have gotten closer to the canyon?' Raja asked.

Chimpu shook his head.

'Arya is right. Rakshasas don't focus on anything to do with nature,' he said half smiling, half sad. 'This unfeeling trait of theirs actually gives us an advantage. Besides, the far side of the canyon that slopes down into the abyss is the only side that is covered with trees, quite thickly too. The rakshasas would not be able to perceive the difference with a few more.'

Yes! I was beginning to feel more confident about our strategy.

'So, when should we plan to go to the far side?' I asked.

'Only the monkeys will descend from the far side, led by the other vanaras. You must enter from here, the steep side, which is closest to the stake. You need to get there at the earliest while the rest of us distract the rakshasas,' Chimpu replied.

No way! I needed to make it down from the ledge along the steep walls of the canyon!

'Chimpu, how? It's impossible!'

'*Plavang*' he responded.

'*Plavang*?'

The direct translation amounted to something like leap or fly out but the last time I leapt into nothingness, I'd ended up freewheeling down the cliff side to this rocky ledge.

'The three of us will help you. We'll take you down to the edge,' Chimpu said. 'But once you reach the mouth of the canyon itself, you'll be on your own. You'll have to lead the battle.'

I gulped. It was all on me now.

'Alright then,' I said, 'when do we begin?'

'Not yet, it's still too dark and rakshasas are more powerful in the hours of darkness. We must wait for total sunlight. It blinds them.'

'How so?'

'Their tawny red eyes can see clearly only in the night light. They are weakened by the powerful glow of the sun. So, daytime gives us an advantage. But, we shouldn't wait until broad daylight to commence our way down. We will start at the call of the leopard.'

'The call of the leopard?'

'Yes, leopards inhabit these clifftops during the hours of darkness. They are nocturnal creatures that eat just about anything they can lay their paws on, which is why it would be dangerous for us proceed at night, especially for our cousins, the lesser monkeys. We have not been gifted with extraordinary night vision like the cats. However, when the leopards retreat to their cave dwellings, they call to mark the daylight hours. That call would be our signal.'

The call of the leopard. This must have been the feline cry I'd heard early that morning. We passed the next few hours on the ledge, strategising further about how to face the rakshasas. A smaller group of vanaras would accompany me, while the rest would encircle the canyon, before making their way down the slope of the far side.

How impressed was I by Chimpu's martial strategy! He was a born general, naturally deft at optimising the use of their survival skills and figuring out how to go from defensive to offensive! Could it have to do with the fact that vanaras descended from the Old World Tribes? If they'd really been around for millions of years, while the earth went through change and evolution, they must have had a lot to contend with. Perhaps they'd endured battles of survival against various animals, and against the earth itself. No wonder they had developed such agility, not to mention the ability to work together.

Even as descendants of the Old World Tribes, we human beings were very different. We rarely pulled together anymore. And when we did, it was only because we were trained to do so in an army boot camp. Moreover, our objective was almost always destructive, rather than constructive, or even defensive.

With just another hour till sunlight, my eyelids drooped, heavy with the weight of the world.

'Rest,' said Chimpu, 'we have some time left.'

So we all settled down, huddled together on the thin ledge. As I wafted into another fitful nap, I couldn't help but go over the events of my journey. It was my fourth day in the Wild Woods. There had to be good reason behind everything I'd experienced since I'd fallen through the fault. One event had naturally led to the next. There must have been a reason I had set fire to the forest in my attempt to kill Baalchorni, even though it had not at all been my conscious plan. Everything made sense now—if Pandu hadn't been injured, I'd never have met the Medicine Woman. And if she hadn't sent me off to look for a plant with no healing power, I'd never have followed the shape-shifting chinkara who eventually led me to release my Ramayana straight into the hands of the dark forces. For the first time, I realised that my journey was not merely about saving the last copy of the book but about facing Ravana himself. But what did facing Ravana have to do with saving Ma? That part I hadn't yet figured out.

~

At the first roar of the leopard, the vanaras began to stir. I was already awake.

'It's time,' Chimpu said, 'we must head down to the Dark Side.'

I locked my arms around his shoulders and perched on his back.

'Hold tight,' the vanara cautioned, 'I will use my tail to grab branches as leverage when I swing down through the rocks.'

And so we began our descent. At times the vanaras were entirely suspended by their tails, at other times by their powerful hands. Slowly, they swerved down the rocks and thin shrubbery, careful not to screech as the thorny branches pierced through their hands and tails. Shrub by shrub and rock by rock, they veered downwards until they finally arrived at the outskirts of Lanka.

The walls of the canyon loomed above on all three sides. An observant eye would have noticed that this slope was more thickly wooded than it had been the previous day. But although the rakshasas had the ability to kill, observing things was not their forte. They were far too focused on the prospect of recreating history based upon their own demonic agenda.

Hanumana!

Guided to the edge of Lanka, I ducked behind a large rock to spy on the rakshasas.

Chimpu, Ranga and Raja all spread out along the canyon walls, also positioning themselves behind smatterings of rock that hid them from immediate view. The other vanaras, hidden behind the tree stumps followed suit, spreading themselves out to cover the walls of the canyons. The monkeys stayed further up on the slope of the far side, ready with their slingshots.

Before us, stretched 400 yards of putrid wasteland with fetid odours evaporating from its marshy floor. The odour was similar to the smell of decaying meat. Interspersed throughout the marsh were large cragged rocks broken up into smaller islands. The wasteland swarmed with red-eyed rakshasas oozing yellow pus and dripping blood from their fangs and talons.

The rakshasas had spent the night preparing for the ritual burning of the epic. The funeral stake was a massive pile of deadwood laden with ghastly looking bones, droppings and foul-smelling flesh of jungle animals. It was built upon an island surrounded by odiferous green marsh and flying rakshasas. How on earth would we cross the ocean of demons to get there?

'Are you ready?' Chimpu whispered from across the canyon wall.

I looked at him with a sense of purpose, raising my brow in anticipation.

'*Plavang*,' I said slowly. 'I would be the first human being to try without a bungee.'

'If my people can do it then yours can too,' Chimpu said. 'Remember, we both descended from the Old World Tribes.'

It was true, but thus far no descendent of the Old World Tribes had been known to *plavang* like Hanumana.

'Reawaken your muscle memory, Arya Vir. Use your limbs in the way your forefathers did.'

Arya Vir. The name rang in my head like a cluster of temple bells. It symbolised everything that I was—my purpose in life, my purpose in the Wild Woods. If I could tap my inner storehouse of energy to truly re-awaken my muscle memory, then this could be my hour of glory.

'The rest of us will wait, watch and then follow,' Chimpu said. He bowed his head respectfully and saluted, like a soldier to his commander-in-chief.

I closed my eyes to plan my next move, while Chimpu prompted the other vanaras to be watchful. They were ready for battle, but needed to take their cue based on my movements.

Once again, I dug deep into my being seeking the energy tunnel that would take me to my root storehouse of Brahman Shakti. As I slowly approached its resting place, I experienced something different than before. My storehouse of energy was deeper this time. More grounded perhaps, than it had been previously. And the deeper I ventured into it, the more ammunition I was able to muster.

An explosion of creation energy at the bedrock of my root emulated that of the silver arrow that had exploded the avalanche the night before. A brilliant light burst out of my body, blue at its core, and white on the outside, with rainbow-coloured rays reverberating from its edges into the rakshasa-scented air.

Something changed inside of me for good. My skin glistened with the essence of creation energy. I was no longer an adolescent boy from San Francisco who had fallen through a fault in the earth, but a warrior who had completed his metamorphosis. My eyes opened to the world, ablaze with rainbow energy. My hair stood up straight and every single muscle was exaggerated. Like the Medicine Woman, I had transformed into my True Self—I feared nothing and I was ready to take on any challenge to fulfil my duties. Arya Vir, the Brave Protector of the People.

The rakshasas stared aghast at the strange aura of blue, white and then rainbow light emanating from the rock formation behind which I had been hiding all this while. But there was no longer any reason to hide. When I stepped forward onto an air cushion to reveal my True Self, they erupted into a torrent of barbaric chaos. I eyeballed them as they turned violent, lashing their tongues and whipping their tails from side to side, as they prepared to attack. A handful of rakshasas charged towards me, spitting venom from their fangs.

Ready to *plavang*. In a single leap, I made it to a rock island in the marsh a few hundred feet away.

The rakshasas rushed forward to ensnare me. Despite being masters of attack, unlike the vanaras, there was nothing strategic about their martial approach. They stopped what they were doing, and ran headlong from wherever they stood to attack me in whatever manner they could. But their collective mismanagement gave me an advantage. Each time they drew near, I leapt to another island. I continued this way from island to island, getting successively closer to the funeral pyre, gaining confidence with each leap.

The rest of the vanaras needed no indication, they began mimicking my actions exactly. Within moments, the marshes of Lanka were transformed into a circus of vanara acrobats. Working in unison, our army succeeded in confusing the rakshasas, making them bolt in every direction.

Then, an uproar arose from the trees. A host of tree stumps fell to the floor and began tumbling down the side of the mountain to reveal an army of monkeys, all strategically positioned down the hillside. The rakshasas, blurred by the barrage of tree stumps bumped and heaved into one another to avoid the tree missiles headed towards them.

Up until now, I had only been exposed to terrestrial rakshasas that could tread the terrible marshy floor. Suddenly, I was faced with an onslaught of flying demons. Looking down upon the canyon the previous day, I had originally taken them to be giant bats. But now it was clear as day that these were winged rakshasas, oozing green pus from their skin and emitting blinding rays of red light from their evil eyes. They approached rapidly from all sides—anywhere I leapt, I was sure to jump headlong into their jaws.

'*Patthar*!' Chimpu called out to the monkeys on the hill.

On cue, they began to throw stones and pebbles in an attempt to blind the rakshasas mid-flight. The rakshasas shrieked before falling to the swamps below, the grimy stickiness oozing from the marshes lodged into their wing spokes. The weight of demoniacal slime prevented them from elevating back into the sky. Within moments, they sank into the marshy floor sucked in by a force that left little chance for survival.

'Down here!' Chimpu commanded his army. In response, they began hurtling pebbles and stones at the terrestrial rakshasas too. Along with this, many grabbed clumps of loose soil, which they released into the air. Slowly, Lanka was filled with a dust storm that blinded the demons.

'Fire. Set it on fire!'

So massive was the voice from somewhere up high that boomed throughout the canyon, I knew it could only belong to Ravana.

The funeral stake was lit, and right in the centre lay my precious Ramayana. Its gilded cover gleamed like a jewelled cat's eye amidst the green flames. With the deepest breath that my lungs would allow, I bounded onto the stake and quickly snatched up the book. I deposited it inside my quiver and sealed the latch tight. Then, I positioned my bow and prepared to string my golden arrow.

The flames sprung up around me, hissing like hot and angry snakes. Peals of vicious demoniacal laughter echoed through the depths of the canyon. The rakshasas everywhere snarled menacingly. Ravana had succeeded in getting me right where he'd wanted. Here, in the middle of the funeral pyre, he intended to burn me along with the troubled epic.

Or so he thought. The voracious flames crept up to lick the outskirts of the aura of rainbow energy that had encircled me. Even after several trials, the flames could not come near me. The epic and I were both safe within the realm of Brahman Shakti. Even the vanaras looked on in disbelief. It was the power of the Agneyasthra! Guru*ji* was a grand master! Endowed with the divine weapon, I was now immune to devastation by fire.

But of course, this wasn't the case for the vanaras, who began to squeal and screech, partly from frustration, partly in fear, and partly from the discomfort of the intense heat.

'Retreat!' I commanded. 'Retreat to the upper side.'

'We cannot leave you!' Chimpu said, as he hopped around in a fluster.

'RETREAT!' I roared. My eyes blazed with the energy of Brahman Shakti.

Chimpu knew he had to obey. Avoiding the clutches of the confused rakshasas, he ordered the vanaras to scamper off one by one up the hillside.

But I quickly caught sight of one vanara that was still leaping around the canyon in frenzy. Why hadn't he retreated to the hillside with the others? Surrounded by the rakshasas who lashed out at him with clubbed limbs and forked tongues, he showed no signs of being afraid. On the contrary, he manoeuvered the marshes with calculated and precise movements. Safe in my rainbow energy, I watched him from a distance. His mischievous smile did not escape my attention.

The vanara swerved towards the demons taunting them, and then, deftly leapt out of their way when they struck.

The ease with which he was teased them left me amazed. It was like this wasn't the first time he'd played games with demons. I didn't recognise him, he definitely was not part of the group I had become so close to over the past four days. He had the look of a mature army general, wisened from years of military practice.

The glow of the fire intensified, and with the higher temperatures surfaced a series of confused roars. The flames began to spread and the terrified rakshasas scurried to flee the fast-spreading flames. There was no camaraderie to be seen, each rakshasa was now concerned only for its own safety. While one attempted to escape, it would invariably step over or injure others on the way.

As the chaos increased, the lone vanara became ensnared in flames. Within moments, his tail was set ablaze. Instinctively, I reached out to help, but stopped when he calmly turned towards me and joined his hands together in a greeting. It was clear that he felt no pain. In that moment he looked regal, celestial almost. With a wave of the paw, he leapfrogged sideways, taking the fire with him.

Immediately I understood that this was no ordinary vanara. It was Hanumana! He *had* come after all. He too, endowed with the Agneyasthra, was immune from destruction by fire. At that precise moment he was doing what he had already done in times past—setting fire to the Lanka with his tail. The only difference was, back then it had been a Lanka signifying the trial of Rama, this time the trial was entirely mine.

I wanted to call out to him but it was a moment for action rather than words. Soon, as the old vanara leapt from hillock to hillock, Ravana's Lanka went up in flames. The rakshasas, terror-stricken by the intensity of the fire, forgot about the Ramayana and its guard "Arya". They simply began to flee this way and that.

Arya of Ravana's Passion

Then came Ravana's voice from somewhere above.

'Let the monkey do as he pleases. Fool, you cannot escape my wrath.'

Way up high, above and beyond the flames that enveloped the canyon, a ball of green incandescence grew out of the space in front of the canyon ridge. In the blink of an eye, it emitted the shape of Ravana, the most hideous rakshasa of all. But, this Ravana looked nothing like the ten-headed demon with multiple arms that I'd expected to see. Nor did he have scales or forked tongues or webbed wings, like the others.

Instead he looked distinctly human—like a large powerful man, in a freshly starched doctor's coat. The doctor...from the hospital in San Francisco! I stood face-to-face with the demon that wanted to kill my mother!

'Pull the plug on her life support,' he said.

'Ravana? Have I known you all along?' I called out to him.

'Indeed,' came the same voice, but this time from behind me. I swung around to find another human-like rakshasa emerging from the green ball of luminosity still suspended before my eyes. Perched on a rocky ledge on the wall of the canyon, this too was Ravana, but vastly different from the last one. I recognised the well-built boy from the schoolyard, perfectly good looking at the first glance, but ugly once he opened his mouth to reveal yellow, crooked teeth.

'What's up scrawny terrorist?' he sneered.

Elias! He had plagued me for months before becoming the reason that led me to reject Ma and ultimately cause her accident. I stared at both Elias and the doctor, wondering how Ravana had the ability to multiply himself.

'Ravana has the ability to be exactly who he wants to be,' the demon's incensed voice responded.

His malicious laughter echoed through the canyon as yet another Ravana emerged from the green ball. This time, it was Athena taunting me with my lunchbox in her hands.

'Goopeater, eating goop! Eating stuff that looks like ...'

'I thought you were Baalchorni,' I interrupted. 'I thought you were dead.'

Her laughter resounded louder and more vile as she was joined by the other two.

'And I thought you were the Ramayana expert,' all the three Ravanas replied in unison.

I was. I didn't need to refer to the book to remember that when Ravana lost one head, he always grew another. I had killed Baalchorni but, of course, it didn't mean anything. She was simply a head that grew back, meaner and uglier than before.

I recalled each line of each verse, each chapter and each page. It was clear to me now that Ravana was everywhere, his heads had manifested themselves as ten different demons in my life. Three had emerged, what about the other seven?

'Look, and you shall find Ravana in every corner of your Lanka,' the rakshasa's voice boomed.

I pivoted in a complete circle, looking to see what else was out there. One by one, out of the green fireball emerged the rest of The Boys. First Zak then Jackson, Jet, Alec and finally Mitch. All five sneered in their usual manner.

'Arya Bin Laden,' Zak called out.

'Goopeater,' Jackson followed.

'Terrorist!' Jet said.

Alec and Mitch just stood there flicking wisps of green rakshasa energy towards me, echoing their friends' words. Goopeater! Terrorist! The slander rang louder and louder in my head.

But for the first time in my life, I wasn't fazed. I continued pivoting around, until I stopped to face the ninth Ravana. Another shape emerged from the green ball to reveal a bony-faced woman looking down disapprovingly at me from a high-collared cloak emblazoned with moons and stars. Jackson's mother, still dressed like an evil witch from the Halloween party. It was hardly a costume.

'Curry-muncher!' she sneered.

Ravana's laughter boomed ominously as I stood firm on the funeral pyre, engulfed by flames that couldn't reach me. I was protected by the power of the Agneyasthra.

Then, to my utter horror, my eyes fell upon the last Ravana, this one was worlds apart—a thin, wiry creature in a black hooded cloak stepped out of the green light and approached directly into my line of vision. The hood reached far enough over its face to shadow its features.

I stood firm, conscious of the rainbow energy spiking around my aura.

'Who is this?' I asked. Ravana's laughter intensified into a cackle.

'Ironic, is it not, that even in the best of moments you cannot recognise yourself?'

His words rattled me. Myself? Impossible!

'Maybe not right now,' boomed Ravana's loud voice 'but once I have completely taken over.' I scrutinised the black-hooded creature cautiously and shook my head.

'Ravana cannot take over an Arya.'

'Why? Are you invincible?'

'Yes, I'm the Protector.'

'What kind of a Protector cannot protect himself?' Ravana said, 'I took over you a long time ago.'

To my utter horror, the last Ravana threw off its cloak to reveal a gut-wrenching reality. Before me stood a twelve-year-old boy with a familiar sulky face, balancing with ease on his blue and yellow skateboard.

I glared at the mirror image of myself—the angry boy from San Francisco, who had rejected his identity. Only one thing was different—his body was translucent, inside it burned the green fire of rakshasa energy, the internal inflammation burning at his...my...core.

To say it was the harshest wake-up call would be a complete understatement. To think that all those years Ravana had controlled me! No wonder, I'd been responsible for Ma's unfortunate accident. Ravana had *wanted* her to die because she had done her bit to kindle the *Rama* inside me, something that was quite the opposite of the demon's master plan. I understood that I had to come face-to-face with the demon. If not, I'd never be able to save myself, let alone Ma, Pandu, the vanaras or the rest of humanity.

Then, I heard Guru*ji*.

'But is it really a mirror image?' his voice boomed out of the darkness, louder even than Ravana's laugh. 'Look at yourself now Arya, look at your True Self. Now tell Ravana, is it a mirror image that you see?'

Was it? Staring me in the face was the image of a shattered boy who had never stood up to the demons, but let them control his life. It was the Arya before he had fallen through the fault in the earth, before he had understood the value of stories from the epic, and before he had begun to understand his true potential. It was Arya's cynical self, his shadow state, the alter ego of his True Self.

'This too is Ravana,' the Guru*ji*'s voice echoed. 'We know him as Arya of Ravana's Passion.'

Arya of Ravana's Passion. The words knifed my core. A few days ago, Guru*ji* had asked me to quell my internal inflammation because he was aware of this demon that it had created. But today, I also knew I *could* quell it because I'd closed the door to this demon. He could no longer control me in my new avatar. As my True Self, the eternal state of my soul, I feared nothing.

Ten different demons pieced the jigsaw together. Ravana had existed as a ten-headed demon for Rama, but for me, he was different. As long as I acceded to evil, this rakshasa of rakshasas would continue to haunt my life.

'Well done, Arya Vir.' Guru*ji*'s voice boomed with resounding approval. It was the first time he had referred to me by name.

'How will you use your final arrow?'

By now I was sure of one thing, I was in no hurry. Nope, I was done with instant reaction. I could overcome these aspects of Ravana but the real question was—how to overcome them all with just one arrow?

'Choose your target carefully,' Guru*ji* advised. 'Wisely. Remember, this is the golden arrow. And gold shines brighter than all other metals.' Ravana's sinister voice rang out into the night, 'Your arrow might be golden, but nothing shines brighter than the energy of Ravana.'

And with that the demons prepared their attack.

Green fire began to emanate from the ten Ravanas encircling my rainbow aura with flames of the rakshasa energy.

I strung the golden arrow to my cast iron bow, pivoting around one last time. I moved very slowly, observing the Ravanas one by one. How I detested that doctor in the white lab coat. So flippant about killing others, he deserved to die. But then there was Athena laughing spitefully as she threw my lunch across the darkness. I watched her morph into the Medusa-like Baalchorni with her serpentine tail and locks. Now was my chance to finish her off for good.

Elias, an enemy that had pretended to be a friend. Should I attack the demon who time and again had been the bane of my existence? The rest of The Boys looked on in sycophantic glee. Zak, Jackson, Mitch, Jet and Alec. All the demons that had been manipulated by Elias stood in front of me. Aiming my arrow at a bunch of sycophants could hardly be the best use of it.

Jackson's mother. The world would certainly be better off without a racist witch like her. But then, my eye caught the black-hooded cloak that lay hovering in the space before my alter ego standing on his skateboard.

The cloak represented the unseen, the evil that potentially lurked in my future. I thought about how often I had been called a 'terrorist'. How befitting a label for a boy should he ever relinquish control to Ravana.

So, I brought the tip of my golden arrow to rest at Arya of Ravana's Passion. *This was my true target,* the other Ravanas paled in comparison.

At that very moment, all the ten Ravanas zoomed in to attack me, each propelled forward by the green fire of the rakshasa energy. It was time.

As I breathed into my belly, I experienced an enormous energy exploding from every living cell of my body. I aimed the arrow at my alter-ego's forehead. Then, shuffling the pages of the Ramayana in my mind, I opened them to the very last portion of the epic—

'Rama stood facing Ravana at the battlefield in Lanka. After shooting several arrows through his heart and each of his heads, Ravana had shown no signs of dying. Instead, his heads had re-grown each time they were being struck, laughing louder with each blow.'

I observed Rama through my mind's eye. I saw him shoot his final arrow at the demon's navel. This was where Ravana's power emanated from. This was his very core. It was what I also needed to do—kill my inner Ravana at its very core.

I caught a glimpse of Hanumana hovering up in the sky. The vanara beamed at me through the intensity of the flames. He raised his big, hairy hand and gestured a thumbs up at me.

'Yes,' he affirmed with just a look into my soul. 'You are doing as Rama would, as he did during another time.'

I smiled recognising the gruff voice and hairy hand of the Headmaster. Hanumana had been with me all along! Things had truly come full circle.

When I released the golden arrow, everything froze around me. There was no action, no sound, no movement. Just a single arrow sailing through the space between two Aryas—Arya Vir, the Brave Protector of the People and the Arya of Ravana's Passion. It sent ripples of rainbow energy moving outwards from its tip and moments later, it pierced the latter directly through the navel.

Arya of Ravana's Passion shattered into a million pieces. As it did, the demon's raucous laughter distorted into a snarling cry. The other nine Ravana figures tottered precariously and then coalesced into a central ball of green flames. Moments later, the green ball morphed into the classical form of Ravana recognisable from the epic—an onerous demon with ten ugly heads, each different from the last. Some bearded, some clean-shaven, some with thick-pointed mustaches. The facial features differed vastly—from the shape of the eyes to that of the cavities in which they were set. But a certain pained expression was common to all of them.

'Do you truly believe that this is the end, Arya?' the demon asked. 'The Dark Forces will meet you again. When man has depleted the resources of his natural habitat, Ravana shall arise, again.'

I stood fearless as the demon disintegrated into the canyon floor. The marshes reverberated with a deafening roar. The ground began to shake, sending thick spurts of green slime and orange flames to engulf the fleeing rakshasas trying to survive the chaos. The walls of the canyon began closing in on me, swallowing the rock islands along with the marshes still swarming with the rakshasas. I needed to make my escape. I scanned the sky for Hanumana, but he was nowhere to be seen. The vanaras had retreated from the lower slopes of the canyon. Many of them had reached the top and were out of danger. They shrieked down at me, terrified perhaps that I'd be consumed by the shrinking canyon.

As the canyon walls moved inwards, the forests on both the edges outside veered closer. Above the tallest trees, I saw the sun, suspended like a golden orb in a sea of azure. Silhouetted against it was the profile of a vanara leaping to the horizon, cushioned by a gust of wind. His tail stood upright, behind bent legs that propelled him forward. His one hand carried an all-familiar club, the other waved at me from the distance. Hanumana! Although I'd wanted to seek him out, I knew he was now journeying back to Vayu's abode. It had been a brief but meaningful encounter. *Plavang*. If Hanumana could do it, so could I! After all, we'd descended from a common ancestor.

The funeral stake on which I stood began to sink into the mouth of the canyon. I grabbed my bow tightly, wondering for a moment what I'd need it for, now that

I had no more arrows. I clung to my quiver with the epic safely nestled inside. And then I leapt for life.

The floor of the canyon opened up and swallowed the stake, the remaining rakshasas and the burning flames of Lanka. Then releasing earth and mud from its interior, the walls of the canyon closed in bringing together the trees that it had once separated.

I landed upon a grassy clearing, on what used to be the northern edge of the canyon. The energy aura around me had disappeared. I looked behind to see the last remnants of Lanka, however there was nothing left to see. No canyon, nor any evidence that there had been one. No cracks, no faults, no mound of earth heaped up to cover the graveyard of rakshasa blood. All that remained was a multitude of fruit trees swaying in the gentle breeze of the morning.

I stood motionless as my army of vanaras jumped down from the trees, chittering, screeching and beating their chests. They cheered, and some kissed their tails in excitement. It was a joyful moment—their task had been completed. Ravana was gone, Lanka was no more and the story of Rama was safe, once again. The monkeys, more jubilant even than the vanaras, played and frisked, swinging high onto tree branches.

It took Chimpu a while to calm things down. He turned to the crowd of monkeys and vanaras.

'Thank you, my brothers. Your efforts have once again helped save the history of our people. Our focus from here on should be home and family. Let no one believe that the Old World Tribes of India can ever become extinct.'

I observed him instruct the simian troops to recoil into the forest.

'Wait,' I said. 'I need to say something.'

Chimpu signalled them to slow down. I cleared my throat.

'Before I came here, I knew about you all from my mother's stories,' I said. 'I was always intrigued by your carefree ways, but never believed that you actually existed. To me, it was some glorified fairy tale about forest monkeys. It didn't occur to me that forest-dwellers like yourselves had the might or the foresight to wage war, and certainly not against demons.'

I paused looking deeply into the faces of the crowds around me.

'Today, I understand why my mother talked about you with such respect. You all stand by your identity, your culture and your people. You risk your lives to save your history from being eroded so you can continue to uphold the flag of Hanumana.'

I paused, joining my hands in the respectful gesture of prayer, before speaking further. 'Thank you for your support in helping me vanquish Ravana, but more importantly, thank you for showing me who I need to be.'

The vanaras began to chitter once again. Touched by my words, they ran up to hug me, and then to my great surprise, they hauled me up on their shoulders.

'*Jai* Arya!' the vanaras echoed in unison. 'Leader of the Old World Tribes.'

The equally touched Chimpu returned the show of respect by joining his hands. 'We vanaras might rapidly shift from one emotion to the next, but when we designate a leader, it is no fickle decision.'

I grinned. It was ironic to be called a leader by those who had taught me so much.

'Come,' Chimpu said, 'Pandu is waiting.'

I nodded. 'But before that, I must pay a quick visit to the Medicine Woman.'

Chimpu was obviously bewildered by this. 'For what? You never did find the Deep Medicine.'

'I did.' I said, happy and excited at once. 'It was in my hands all the time. Trust me, we won't be late for Pandu.'

The Backwaters—Again

The Medicine Woman was seated on a hillock overlooking the black stream. A series of waterfalls flowed behind her, creating a multitude of rainbows as the droplets caught the sun's rays. A misty halo engulfed her presence resembling the ring around the moon on a foggy night.

Steeped in meditation, she sat upright in lotus pose, her eyes closed and her long black hair waving around her torso. She held a golden sieve on one hand and waved it towards the rainbow. She motioned with her other hand to gather particles of the multi-coloured arc through her golden sieve. Completely elated, I burst through the distance with lightning speed and fell abruptly at her feet, while Chimpu held back at the trees. 'You knew about it all before it even happened, didn't you?' My voice echoed through the valley forcing her out of her trance.

The Medicine Woman opened her eyes and smiled, her serene face etched with wisdom.

'You were the moonlight that lit my path through the forest that night,' I continued. 'You were with me *all* the time.'

'As I will be,' she replied, 'always.' I paused, dazzled by all the seven colours of the rainbow, that reflected on her raven black hair. She radiated with the essence of an angel.

'There is no plant in the forest with no medicinal value,' I said with absolute certainty.

She laughed, tilting her head to one side.

'My child, then you have learned your lesson well.'

How many times had I heard these familiar words? As I looked into her changing eyes, I recognised the wise counsel of my mother. How had I not known this from the outset?

'Ma? Is it really you?'

'My son, it is.'

In that moment, the reason for my journey became clear. It wasn't about the medicinal plant, and perhaps it wasn't about the medicine at all. I'd come to see Ma, to reconcile myself with the reality that here in the Backwaters, she was not a helpless woman strapped up to life-support systems, but had found her True Self, free of the scars that had haunted her since that fateful day in Chinatown.

'The Deep Medicine is the Ramayana, isn't it?' I asked, eager for approval.

She replied, 'Yes, Arya. It was in your hands all along.'

'So I must read father these verses, just as you've always read them to me,' I said, with new understanding.

'And watch him reawaken to a happier world.'

The Ramayana gleamed in the light of the rainbows.

She laughed gently, radiating warm vibrations that cocooned me in an aura of true happiness. 'And what do you make of it now, Arya?'

'That Ravana exists in me if I let him, and without vanquishing my own inner demons, I could never heal or protect, or be the person you named me for.'

She took my hand and held it tightly in her own. 'See Arya, aren't we all saved by what we learn in the land of the Ramayana?'

I nodded. This is what she had taught me all along.

'Ma, where do I go from here?' I asked.

'Home, to a father who needs you,' she responded.

Deep in her kaleidoscopic eyes, I saw my father gazing sadly at my indisposed mother. For the first time, I had a strong feeling that it was no longer necessary to save her. The essence of the Ramayana existed in her True Self. My journey was nearing its end.

I blinked my eyes back into the moment. 'Is this where we say goodbye?' I asked.

The Medicine Woman looked at me with an expression that defined love better than anything I'd ever read in a book or seen in a movie. It was an expression that would stay with me for years after, imprinted in my memory.

'Arya,' she said. 'Let your conscious mind retain the image of that moonlight guiding you through the path in the scary jungle. I will always be there to show you the way, but you must face life's challenges on your own.'

I thought about the days following the accident; when I'd longed for Ma to return from her stillness. Waiting had been traumatic, or so I thought at that time. But today I realised that it had been part of her master plan. Had she woken up from her coma, this journey would not have taken place. So she lay still, deriving breath through an oxygen mask. I had finally learned how to fight like a warrior, but truth be told, Ma had been the real warrior all along. I'd been living in denial all this time, detesting the thought of the life-support equipment, rejecting anything that reminded me of her. Although Pa had practically begged me, I refused to accompany him to the nursing home. All that rejection was because somewhere deep inside, I'd given up hope that I could ever see her again—alive and happy as she had once been.

But the day I chanced upon her copy of the Ramayana, everything changed. The gilded writing on its leather cover glimmered in the darkness with hope for her survival. Little did I know then that I'd also discovered the key to my own survival.

I glanced around at the magnificent panorama of rainbows set against the waterfalls.

'I'm sorry about the graffiti, that day outside Rainbow grocery. I can see now that I was vandalising a picture of your home in the Backwaters.'

As she smiled in response, against the waterfalls, more beautiful than ever, I knew she would always be my guardian angel. I was finally ready to say goodbye.

I bent down to touch her feet and seek her blessing, she returned the gesture by placing her fingers on the crown of my head.

As she brought me up to a standing position, a ray of lambent sunlight broke through the bands of a rainbow scattering an array of colour into a halo around the two of us. She snapped something out of the brilliant dispersion and placed it in my hands.

'What's this?' I asked looking into a small piece of graphite rock that shimmered with the blush of seven shades.

'Quantum energy, the spell conjured by the other side of the rainbow.'

Deep in her eyes, I caught a glimpse of that other side. It was a teaser, gone in a flash before my mind could register the details. Somewhere in time though, I knew I would get there.

'*Ayushmaan bhava*, Arya,' she whispered. 'May you live as long as you can protect your race.'

Then, with one last meaningful peek at the Medicine Woman, I turned to make my way towards Chimpu. Together, we began to retrace our steps through the forest. I heard her call out behind me—'Invoke your inner energy, Arya. It will stand you through the test of time.'

Her words were arrows to my soul. But I didn't need to stop or turn around. The image of my mother's True Self propelled me on to my future.

Home

The verses of the Ramayana healed Pandu's burns in no time. When we finally arrived by his side, he could scarcely open his eyes, but by the time I was close to narrating the last few chapters, he was sitting up and listening intently, still pale but with hints of colour returning to his cheeks. All the other vanaras fussed around him, relieved to see their companion returning to health.

They recounted for Pandu, with most vivid detail, all that had come to pass with Ravana and the rakshasas of the Dark Side. But while the indisposed vanara had missed it all, his delirium had brought on visions of all that had happened.

'I saw Ravana go down,' he said. 'I saw the earth swallow him up in her jaws, along with the entire band of evil rakshasas who had plagued The Wild Woods for many seasons.'

Buddha, who hadn't heard the full story yet wanted to make sure it wasn't a fever-driven hallucination. 'Who made this vision possible?' he asked.

'Guru*ji*,' Pandu replied. 'He showed me how Arya had sent the rakshasas once again to the depths of the earth.'

At the mention of the Guru*ji*, Buddha knew it was true. The weight of a hundred years lifted from his shoulders.

Guru*ji* had once again performed his magic. Shortly after Chimpu and I left in search of the Deep Medicine, he had drawn out a vision cloud in the open sky around Pandu to broadcast our adventures. Those vanaras who had stayed behind to nurse him had seen everything unfurl like a movie on a massive screen. And Pandu had seen it in his unconscious state.

'Guru*ji*,' I said, reflecting on his tactics. 'He is certainly the master of his game.'

'One could perhaps say the same about you, Arya,' came an old familiar voice. It was the master himself.

A cloud of blue energy appeared out of nowhere. Guru*ji* sailed through its centre, balanced in Virbhadrasana, the warrior position that Yoga gurus tout as the first order of mental and physical discipline. He landed on the ground before us and slowly came out of the posture, waving his golden staff. I noticed how he wielded it like a weapon.

'A weapon it is,' Guru*ji* affirmed. 'Though, less for my own defence and more for that of others.' I tossed the idea around in my head.

'How did you become so well-versed in martial arts?' I asked.

Guru*ji*'s eyes sparkled with nostalgia. He brandished his staff slicing the airspace before him into pieces. 'I too, was a Protector of my people,' he said. 'But with a different objective. I was a king once, competitive in my youth, and filled with ego. I had an unending desire to conquer the universe by imposing my power over others.'

I remembered Ma's words. 'Kings are like lions, creatures of pride, who need to protect their territory.'

'Rightly so,' Guru*ji* said. 'But, there is a vast difference between protecting one's territory and becoming territorial.'

'So, you are a *rajarshi*,' I said. 'A royal saint.'

'I'll admit it wasn't easy to relinquish the ways of a warrior,' Guru*ji* said, 'and there are still days when I miss heading out with my war cry. But after a certain point in time, even a warrior must lay down his weapons for good.'

My mind went back to Ma. She was a warrior too, fighting for life in the nursing home. It was time for her to lay down her weapons too.

'These forests have been home to mankind for thousands of years. I chose to seclude myself to its remotest parts for years; to pay penance for the atrocities that I'd committed before.'

'It must have been a hard price to pay,' I remarked.

'It was,' Guru*ji* replied. 'Imagine the willpower needed to trade your weapons for a sage's staff.'

'No wonder you were the ideal guru for Rama.'

'Your training is at a nascent stage, Arya. The values of a warrior and the trials of our times have only just begun to make sense to you.'

The twinkle in Guru*ji*'s eye gave way to a deep, yet, heartwarming smile, his face wrinkled with the wisdom of a 1, 000 years.

'Arya,' Guru*ji* asked gently, 'are you ready to go back home?'

Was I? I first glanced at Guru*ji*, at the distant hills of the Wild Woods, and then at the vanaras gathered nearby. As strange as my adventures had been, I'd developed a sense of comfort here—an affinity for the land that offered a life and a longing, so different to the vast shades of grey that had haunted my existence in San Francisco. In just five days, I'd grown to love my new friends, the vanaras; I'd developed an inner security after reuniting with my mother's True Self, and I'd come to respect Guru*ji* and his wisdom.

'But most importantly, you have learned the value of the Ramayana,' Guru*ji* said. 'This ancient epic is the key to becoming schooled in the ways of a warrior.'

Being in the Wild Woods had taught me to quell my inner inflammation and stand up to demons, should they ever dare to show their face. Never again could I let go of these stories. I had a different perspective now, one of a boy who had journeyed through winds of change—a boy who now knew how to tap his Brahman Shakti when the world sent evil his way.

But, was I ready to journey home? Sure, I needed to see my father again, and bring the sunshine back into his life. I needed to head back to the Golden Gate Park to skate my way fearlessly among The Boys. I needed to sail through those lunch hours without shying away from the food of my culture. And, I needed to be there when they pulled the plug on Ma. Yes, I was ready.

'It takes an Arya, you know,' the Guru*ji* said, 'to prevent Ravana from re-writing history, not simply during the chapter of your journey, but through all the chapters of time. Congratulations on arriving at the end of your first *chapter*.'

Ma had always said that only in reaching the end is it possible to start a new beginning. It might have been the end of a chapter in my personal book, but I had an inkling that the bulk of stories were yet to unfold.

'Perhaps, one day you will write them yourself,' said Guru*ji*, waving his staff to release particles of blue Brahman Shakti into the surrounding atmosphere. He gleamed like the golden staff in his hand. And so did I. Like Guru*ji*, I too had grown to love the notion of *perhaps*.

I walked up to each of the vanaras, bidding each of them goodbye. Finally, I gave Chimpu the warmest hug.

'Your vanara sena will be here for you whenever you need it,' Chimpu said. I squeezed his hand in gratitude. There was nothing I needed to say in words. Upon turning to look for the Guru*ji*, I could only discern his dark blue outline silhouetted against the brilliant stream of light. I bent down to touch his feet in respect. As he brought me up to my feet, he waved his golden staff once again to release a shimmer of the brilliant blue energy. My empty quiver and cast iron bow were sucked back into the flash.

'You won't need these,' Guru*ji* said. 'Not for a while.'

He was right. The Ramayana was all I needed back at home.

'That, and a piece of quantum energy. *Ayushmana bhava*, Arya,' echoed the voice of Guru*ji*. 'Continue your journey, until we meet again.'

Until we meet again. It would certainly happen, somewhere in time.

I walked over to an old banyan tree and seated myself at the base of its trunk. Then, with the composure of a sage, I held the book tightly to my chest and began to chant its final verses.

'As long as man continues to walk upon earth, the story of Rama shall be chanted...'

The familiar blue light of Brahman Shakti took shape at my root. With the speed of a jet stream, it zoomed up my central energy tunnel, and burst through the top of my head. The blue sky shook with the electrifying power of creation energy that carried me upwards through the tree branches and out into a dimension beyond space, time and physics.

~

I entered a darkness that soon morphed into the portal that had first brought me to the Wild Woods. A series of hallucinatory images took shape around me, sketching scenes of my journey—the vanaras, Baalchorni's assault, the rakshasas of the Dark Side, the Medicine Woman, Guru*ji* levitating above the canyon, the vivid scenery of the Backwaters and so on.

As I waded my way through the portal, bits and pieces of things that floated up in the same direction surrounded me. At first, it was hard to discern what these were, but soon I began to identify the furniture and accessories from my bedroom that had also fallen through the fault. My desk, my chair, my bookshelf laden with zoology books and everything else. My prized skateboard floated before my eyes, its spinning wheels indicating its readiness for a ride, and my school backpack goading me on to get back to regular life. Within moments, the furniture and I were both sucked up through the open fault. I landed with a thud in my bed, my head covered with white sheets.

As I pulled the sheets down to take a look around, I saw that everything in my room was in perfect order, as though nothing had happened at all. Something distinctly hard jutted out from under my pillow. The Ramayana. Next to it sat a small piece of graphite shimmering with all the seven colours of the rainbow. I picked them up and quietly walked out of the door and down the hallway. When I arrived at mother's prayer room, I placed the book where it belonged. I picked up her string of rudraksha beads and set it along with the graphite rock on top of the book. Then, I returned to my own room. As I nestled my head back in my pillow, I listened quietly to the sounds of the Pacific Ocean beating against the shores of my world.

~

'Goopeater!' Athena squealed as soon as she saw me confidently stride into the lunchroom, the next day. She made her way over to my end of the long lunch table.

I took a bite of khichdi and chewed thoughtfully before responding.

'Can I offer you a taste of my lunch, Athena?' I asked. 'It might help alleviate the indigestion that is responsible for your rotten mood each day.'

'Eat goop?' Athena asked with a scornful expression. 'The terrorist wants me to eat his goop!'

But of course, there was no point in reacting. I'd learned that the battle of good versus evil was a constant tug-of-war. Both aspects existed only to give meaning to the other. Ravana could never completely disappear from existence or else "good" would no longer have meaning. Life was a myriad of experiences. Some good, some bad, and others that made no sense at all. However, over time, even the most nonsensical things would make perfect sense. This was the beauty of life and so I smiled at Athena, victorious in my state of calm.

~

Instinct told me I could find The Boys by the mural in the schoolyard. When I made my way over, all six of them greeted me with snarling expressions.

'The terrorist thinks he's some big shot!' Elias remarked with a smirk.

'Why?' I asked, not sure what he meant.

'How'd you explain that?' Elias asked, pointing his finger towards the mural wall. I turned to see that an Asian boy with dark hair and tan coloured skin had been painted into the picture. The wall smelled of fresh, wet paint, a telling sign that the artist had just completed his work.

After all these years, somebody in the school administration had finally embraced my identity, and now there I was, firmly established upon the wall! But, Elias quickly interrupted my train of thought.

'Got balls, terrorist?'

'Depends,' I replied, nonchalantly.

'On what?' Conner asked.

'On what you have to offer,' I replied.

Elias looked at Mitch. 'Show the terrorist what we got to offer.'

Mitch pulled out a bottle of blue spray paint from his school daypack and waved it in front of my face, 'If you got balls, then graffiti out the Brownie.'

Recalling the events of my last day in the Wild Woods, I knew that when demons approached, a warrior must remain grounded and firm. Only then will those demons abscond.

So, I signalled back to Mitch with a thumbs down.

'I got balls, but spraying graffiti on the mural would be a pretty un-ballsy thing to do.'

The Boys looked at each other, puzzled.

'Not like you haven't done this kind of thing before. So, what's your point, Brownie?' Mitch asked.

I observed the mural carefully.

'Brown's a pretty good colour, don't you think?' I replied. 'It provides definition to the other colours on the canvas. Makes them look less washed out, less run-of-the-mill.'

'Quit the fancy wordplay,' Elias said, annoyed. 'If you don't graffiti out that terrorist kid, then you don't get to race with us on Sunday.'

I raised an eyebrow in curiosity. It was news to me that I even had an opportunity to race with them.

'Sunday?' I asked.

'Against the East side dudes,' Jackson said.

The "Brownie" on the mural sparkled in the sunlight. I knew it was profound in every which way; a portrait not just of myself, but my entire race.

'That boy's fearless,' I said. 'No amount of graffiti can change that.'

Elias became impatient.

'Graffiti the mural, or race with us on Sunday?'

'Race with you, for sure,' I said. 'But the deal is that the mural stays as is.'

The Boys gandered at each other, flabbergasted.

'I ain't strikin' any deal,' Elias said, seething.

'Then, I guess you'll lose,' I replied with a grin. 'Cos you know, you can't win that race without me.'

The truth of my words shocked Elias into submission. He backed away from the mural followed by his entourage.

'You sure got balls,' he said, making his way towards the school building. 'Welcome back, Arya.'

'Thanks Elias,' I replied, grinning. 'It is good to finally arrive.'

I watched as the demons retreated into the shadows of the schoolyard.

~

The school bell rang in the distance, but I had one more stop to make before attending class that afternoon. I raced to the gym.

I spied the janitor's cart sitting in the middle of the room, but I found nobody standing by.

'Niklas?' I called out, surveying all the four corners.

'May I help you?' an unfamiliar voice answered from behind. I turned to see a bald, fat man outfitted in overalls, making his way over.

'I'm looking for the janitor,' I replied.

'That would be me,' the man said.

'But, I'm looking for Niklas. Where is he?'

'He's done,' the new janitor said. 'Finished his contract. I don't suppose he'll be back too soon.'

'Did you need something?' he asked, looking at me suspiciously.

'No,' I replied. 'Well, actually yes. I wanted to know who painted the image of the Asian boy on the mural outside.'

The janitor laughed and shook his head from side to side.

'I get your drift now,' he said. 'Niklas did that. His last piece of work before he left.'

Of course, Niklas was the artist! I'd been witness to Guru*ji*'s paintings on the thin-air canvas of the Wild Woods, but this time, he had created a masterpiece.

'Thank you,' I said, my head pulsating with the colours of a thousand rainbows. 'That's all I needed to know.'

I took off for class, grinning from ear to ear.

~

At dinner, Pa was quiet for the longest time. Finally he spoke, taking his head in his hands.

'Maybe, living with the memory of her good times is better than hoping endlessly for her to wake up, Arya,' he said.

I put my hand on his shoulder. 'It is time to let go, isn't it?'

Pa placed his hand on mine. 'It's not what I'd wanted Arya, but the truth is, I don't know whether she's ever coming back to us.'

I was calm. 'She will,' I said. 'Somewhere in time.'

He looked at me with an odd expression, as though it was the first time he'd ever laid eyes on me. He was trying to figure out who I was.

'You've grown up overnight,' he said.

I had. I gave him a bear hug.

The nursing staff said that it wasn't necessary for the family to be present when they disconnected the life-support system, but both Pa and I wanted to be there.

I decorated Ma's room with clusters of jasmine flowers. She'd always associated its sweet scent with her younger days in India. So when her oxygen mask came off, I wanted her to leave her body inhaling the fragrance of home. Pa was more stoic. He stood by her bed, watching without utterance, marvelling at everything I did. I placed her Ramayana by her pillow with a single twig of jasmine blossoms. Though the sourcebook marked the endpoint of her journey, it also gave hope for another beginning.

The doctor turned to Pa.

'Are you ready?' he asked.

Pa nodded and closed his eyes as the doctor unplugged the machine. My eyes were fixed on the heart-rate monitor. Nothing happened for a minute or two but then the jagged curve marking her heartbeat flattened out into a straight line, the regular beep-beep from the sound machine transformed to a continuous shrill.

But there was no reason to be alarmed. Ma was at peace in the Backwaters.

~

Over the next few days, I watched my father sink to new depths of sadness. Lighting Ma's funeral pyre was particularly hard for him. Although his objective had been to reach closure, it wasn't clear to me whether Pa had made peace with his decision. He couldn't see perhaps that in releasing Ma from life, he'd given her the opportunity to live once again in a different realm, beyond the superficial sensations of pleasure and pain of the earthly world. She could now experience true bliss.

As we stood facing each other across the flames of her funeral pyre, I watched Pa's stoicism translate to bitter weeping. It could only be a good thing—releasing emotion was the first step towards healing. Pa was in need of Deep Medicine, and luckily, I had the ability to help.

After the funeral, we returned to an empty house. Pa wandered into the prayer room and sank down at the altar table. I followed. I lit a clay lamp, easing the darkness of the lonely evening, and pulled out the copy of my Ramayana.

'Would you like to visit the places Ma etched into my mind?' I asked, opening the first page of the book.

Pa nodded feebly.

'Are you ready for the journey?' I asked.

'Yes, my son,' he replied, uncertain about the meaning of my words.

A warm sensation of blue energy began to vibrate at my core as I stepped into my mother's role.

'Once upon a sunny morning in the forests of ancient India, a wise old sage chanced upon the lilting music of two birds. As he listened to their birdsong, patterned in regular metre, he discovered the fascinating adventures of an Arya ...'

And so, I began my story.

Acknowledgements

To say that this book was entirely my own doing would be a gross misrepresentation of facts—the blood and sweat put into the development of this story has come from far and wide.

I'd like to thank Ilya, Arya and Neeraj for dealing with my quirks and mood swings as I wrote the manuscript;

Holly Payne and the Skywriters—Lisen Stromberg, George Grenley and Louise Henrikson for workshopping this story from conception of the idea to a first-draft manuscript;

Lewis Buzby, Masie Cochran, Catherine Frank, Sonalini Choudhary and Ipshita Mitra, your invaluable energy has greatly helped in improving the manuscript;

Solange Langenfeld, your encouragement helped me keep my faith during the difficult phases of writing the story.

Shobha Nihalini, for encouraging me to contact Kanishka Gupta;

Kanishka Gupta, for being the agent who did the trick!

Rakhee Grover Jain, for helping me find those who valued this story enough to promote it;

Kirron Kher, for your invaluable endorsement;

Sally Goldman, the real reason I fell in love with the Ramayana;

My late grandfather, guide and ultimate role model, Gopal Krishan Vij, you live forever in my thoughts;

All the bullies out there—without you this story would be impossible.